STAR FORGED

ASCENSION GATE BOOK 1

JUSTIN SLOAN

ELDER TREE PRESS

Thank you team!

Editors

Myra Shelley

JIT/BETA

Edward Rosenfeld

Lois Haupt

Kelly O'Donnell

Tracey Byrnes

WELCOME

BE PART OF THE GROUP!

Want to never miss one of my releases? Join my newsletter and you'll also get an **EXCLUSIVE BOXSET**, which includes several stories from my series that you can't find anywhere else.

SIGN UP HERE

And join the FB group!
https://www.facebook.com/groups/JustinSloan/

Thank you for taking a chance on my books. I hope you love reading them as much as I loved writing them!

Justin Sloan

1

TRENT: EARTH, KENNEDY SPACE CENTER

Nothing could've excited Trent Helms more than the gateway as it opened in the stars above. This was it—the moment he'd been training for, the moment that pulled his entire future together. He and the other Space Fleet Marines gathered with officers and senior NASA officials, watching as purple and blue light flowed through space like a door to heaven.

They'd opened this particular door before for testing and probes, and while no images had made it back, readings had. Results indicated at least one potentially habitable planet in what they'd named the Krastion Galaxy. This information was enough that, on this night, Trent and the other teams would be the first humans through. They'd be the first to investigate the other side, to learn if there was indeed another option for expanding beyond the Solar System.

And maybe, if they were lucky, they'd discover signs of life.

"I hope you have your big-kid undies on, Gunnery Sergeant," Colonel O'Donnell said, a grin spreading across her normally stern face as she slapped Trent on the shoulder. "I almost shat myself just looking at that thing. Imagine actually flying through it."

"An image I'm sure to carry with me through the gate, sir," he replied with a chuckle. "But we won't have to imagine flying through the gate for long. I want to be the first ship through."

"Damn right," she said. "I take care of mine, just remember that. You and me, we'll shove the rest of them aside if we have to."

He laughed. "Whatever it takes, sir."

She nodded again before moving off to schmooze with one of the politicians in attendance. The woman had high aspirations, which were really the only reasons she had signed up for this mission, Trent assumed. As fun as she could be, he knew it was all part of the role she played. All part of the job. He had aspirations, but only so far as they allowed his advancement with the Space Fleet Marines. He longed to explore space, to be a part of history, and to make a difference.

He imagined they wouldn't need to continue terraforming Titan and Mars if this worked out. Stopping such operations would mean a wealth of resources unspent and much earlier colonization if there were inhabitable planets out there. Not that it was all bad. Such operations on Mars had led to the discovery of this gateway, for instance.

The light finished forming in the sky and a cheer rose up from the crowd, causing Trent to glance over to the media representatives who were capturing it all. Seeing them reminded him of all the people around the world who'd be watching as the teams went through the gate—his dad, for one. He loved the man but hadn't seen enough of him lately. And thinking of his father got him wondering who else might be watching. Perhaps old high school buddies would be among the crowd, as well as the ones who had always looked down on him. Maybe even a certain woman he'd been through so much with—too much, perhaps—would be watching. Shrina Collins. The woman who, in some ways, was largely responsible for him being there today.

Years after their initial meeting in Quantico, she'd shown up one day at an embassy in Rome and gotten him involved in the takedown of Space

Station Horus and their super-soldier program. If not for their involvement, the united governments wouldn't have been able to take over the program, and this mission might have been deemed too risky. Sending regular men and women through a gateway to the stars was one thing, but sending genetically engineered warriors capable of enhanced speed, super strength, and healing—that was another matter altogether. Even if the situation went south, they had a better chance of survival. Hostile aliens, if they existed, would have a tough time against these devil dogs.

All of that had to do with his breakup from Shrina years ago. He hadn't had it in him to tell her that he intended to volunteer for the enhancements, and he knew she wouldn't approve, especially since her sister had seen first-hand how those early attempts at modifications had failed. When Space Station Horus was being run by New Origins, they'd created super soldiers that not only had their minds partially wiped but suffered from periodic loss of control. The government had since revamped the program, seeing to it that these attempts at control and loss of freedom were taken away, and that no rage-related faults continued.

Two Marines approached, laughing, but slowed at the sight of him standing there alone. He wished they'd keep moving, especially considering that one of them was Enise, his most recent fling and, yes, a rebound after realizing he wasn't quite over Shrina. The relationship had helped him, and he'd begun to think that maybe he'd moved on. He'd even considered that she could be *the one*.

That all changed when he'd found out she was sleeping with Staff Sergeant Mercer—the asshole standing with her now. Mercer was grinning at Trent as if all of that had been erased simply because they were going into space together.

"We're finally making it happen," Enise said, beaming.

"Into the great unknown," Trent replied with a polite nod to Mercer. A punch to the throat would've been more appropriate and satisfying, but he knew better than to assault his fellow Marines, especially when he had such high hopes of rising up in the Space Fleet Marines. Besides, this was for the best, he often told himself. Why distract himself with relationship issues when he wanted to be the top of the top? Instead, he focused on his training and preparing for their journey.

And he was ready.

"You tell your pilot to stay out of our way," Trent said with a grin. "I plan on being the first person on planet. I'm gonna be the first to taste that sweet air and take a piss on its soil."

"A lovely sentiment," Mercer said, his smile fading into a frown as if he'd just remembered who Trent was. He was likely drunk, as he often was.

Trent had confronted Enise about the man's drinking problem more than once, but she waved it off, as if doing so could make it go away. She was smart, though, and knew what she was involved with and what she'd done. Trent imagined it might even be her way of dealing with her guilt over cheating on him, like she deserved no better. It wasn't Trent's place anymore, so he left it alone. But if the son of a bitch ever hit her, Trent would be waiting to throttle him.

An awkward silence passed between them and Trent thought they were about to walk off, giving him freedom, when Captains Aarol and Thomas approached, all grins. Both were pilots, and the blue-wing symbols on the shoulders of their space fleet armor were prominently displayed. This reminded Trent of his ultimate goal—go the officer route, become a captain, and fly in the next mission. All of that, of course, would come after he'd proven himself in this first mission through the gate.

Aarol had that quarterback confidence to him, with his perfect hair combed over in a wave.

Thomas was African-American and had a nerdy look to him, one that he often overcompensated for by hanging out with Aarol.

"Tell her no, Helms," Aarol said with a chuckle, seeing them together. "Three-ways with exes? Never a good idea."

"Trust this guy. He knows." Thomas laughed, then gave his buddy a quick nut-check. They both laughed as his metal glove clinked against Aarol's metal crotch.

"We get it, sir, nut protection is great," Trent said, annoyed at their joke at his expense and the way these captains acted like young teens. It was the way they were, though—two frat boys who'd never grown up.

"Great until you try to have that three-way," Aarol said with a nod back to Enise. "These suits are a bitch to remove."

"Sirs," Mercer said with a frown, "this conversation isn't exactly appropriate."

"We're going to space," Aarol said, grinning widely. "Who cares what's what here on Earth? Do you understand, Staff Sergeant, what we're all about to accomplish?"

"It's the ultimate orgy of the universe," Thomas answered, hands in the air. "Just without all the nudity and sex and all that."

"Gentlemen," Mercer said, putting a hand on Enise's back and guiding her away. She gave Trent a glance that said she felt bad, or maybe she was wishing she could have that three-way. Who knew? Trent wouldn't put it past her, not anymore. He didn't think much would be below sleeping with Mercer, after all.

"Lock it up," the colonel said, stopping on her way to another politician. "Head over for final suit checks. We're about to make history."

"Roger that," Trent said, glad to be done with all of them so he could focus on the mission. He understood that teamwork was important, but if he had his way, he'd go it alone. He wasn't a pilot and wasn't the best at flying these new exploration cruisers, but he had learned enough to get by. In fact, he had joined wanting to be a pilot and get fast-tracked through one of the officer programs. But the calls he'd arranged from his old ambassador friend hadn't cut it, apparently, since they'd passed him over for others who better excelled at portions of the test.

He'd been one of the top fighters in both hand-to-hand combat and marksmanship, so they made him Space Fleet Infantry. "Hey, good SFI try," the joke went for those who'd be flying and were dicks enough to rub in the fact that others wouldn't be. It implied that infantry weren't smart enough to make it, while in reality many had been passed over for things like poor vision, their ability to focus under extreme movement tests, and the like.

In what felt like consolation, they'd trained him as an emergency combat medic and taught him to test for air and soil quality. Because of this training, he'd be in the lead, ensuring that the test results from drones were accurate and looking out for any threatening life forms.

Men and women stood in a line, checking the plating and internal tubing on their suits. An inspection team went over weapons and the built-in computers and analysis tools, and then gave them the final permission to set off.

Stopping by Sergeant Espinoza and Corporal Brown, Trent gave them a nod and asked if they were ready.

"Born to kill," Corporal Brown said.

"We're not going up there to kill," Trent replied with a frown. "Just to be clear."

"Says you," Brown replied, tapping the DD4 assault rifle at his side. "This bad boy says otherwise."

"Don't know what we'll meet up there, Gunny," Espinoza added, staring up at the sky. "I just hope Captain Thomas—"

"You're with Thomas?" Trent asked.

"That's right," Espinoza replied.

"When we heard Gunnery Sergeant Tracey Ellins would be in his ship, we made the request," Brown added. "Er, not that we wouldn't have loved to be on your team, Gunny. It's just that—"

"Hey, hey," Trent said, waving the comment off. "I get it. Gunnery Sergeant Ellins, the legend of Dubai." He laughed, then winked as he said, "If I could demote myself to serve under her, you think I wouldn't?"

"You were involved in all that, too, weren't you?" Espinoza asked.

Trent nodded but didn't add any more to it. He was reminding himself that he was the gunnery sergeant in this little group, and it was best not to get into bragging or gossip.

"Well, it's not 'all that' for me anyway," Espinoza added. "Ellins was a Staff Sergeant when I was stationed in Korea, the kind to look out for her team. I've heard good things about you, but I know first-hand she'd tear an alien's head off and spit down its throat before letting one of them so much as mad-dog me. It's that kind of loyalty that'll never go away, you know?"

"And I'm pretty sure he has a crush on her," Corporal Franco added, stepping up to join them.

Trent scrunched his nose at Franco. The guy was

a loose cannon and had been a corporal twice now. The last time, he'd only been a corporal for a week before facing harassment charges and then assault on the guy who'd accused him. It hadn't helped that Franco had been drunk on base while under the legal drinking age. As stupid as Trent felt rules like underage drinking were when applied to the military, he thought a Marine needed to know how to follow rules. If the rules weren't followed, people could die.

While Trent had been lost in thought, Espinoza was busy defending himself, blushing as he tried to convince the other two that he had no crush on anyone going to space with them.

Trent meandered off and found his place in line for an equipment check, wondering what it would've been like to go to space as a corporal. Back then, he was still aspiring to embassy duty and still fawning over Shrina Collins, though he'd barely gotten to know her. When she later showed up in his life, it had been a pleasant surprise.

With a sigh, he pushed such thoughts from his mind, wondering what it was about preparing to fly off to space that made him start rehashing the past. There'd be plenty of time for all that once they had a colony set up. At that point he could decide if he wanted to stay up there. Maybe he *would* stay, and maybe he'd talk to Ellins some more, see what her deal was. Or perhaps he'd eventually find his way back to Earth and be done with all this. Then, maybe he'd look up Shrina.

Knowing his luck, she'd be married and have kids by then, and he would have missed his chance. Maybe it would be a big deal if it happened that way, but at the moment he couldn't allow himself to miss out on this mission.

"Gunny Helms," Corporal Kim said, and Trent turned to see her directly behind him in line. She was a nice girl but sometimes a little too nice. With her straight black hair often tied back and the way her eyes always seemed slightly mischievous, he wouldn't have minded the occasional flirtation she shot his way if he were younger and didn't outrank her. Fraternization wasn't a rule to mess around with.

"Ready to make our dreams come true?" he asked, instantly feeling stupid for saying it that way.

She gave him a confused smile, but said, "I can't believe it's finally happening."

As Corporal Kim spoke, Sergeant Belmes approached and stood nearby, awkwardly, not even turning to acknowledge Trent.

"I remember watching that princess-in-space movie as a little girl," Kim said. "Singing along and imagining myself up there. I'd pretend I was flying around with thrusters and laser shooters, saving my little pet furry. You see that one?"

"Not that I recall," Trent said, glancing over at Belmes, who brightened up at his glance. "You?"

"My twin sis loved it," Belmes said. "I was more of a 'Blade of the Sea' kinda kid. Loved that movie with a passion… you know, until I grew up."

"You're never too grown up to like those movies," Kim said. She turned back to Belmes with a raised eyebrow. "I didn't know you had a twin."

Trent was called forward, glad to leave the conversation behind. As much as he cared for each of these Marines and would give his life for them in combat, right then he wanted to enjoy the moment without the interruption of small talk.

Since there were no issues with either his suit or his gear, he was approved and given permission to head over to the launch field. The moment had finally come, and Trent was near the lead just behind the colonel as they approached their ships. Seeing the gateway above while walking toward the ship that would take him through it was a different experience altogether. This was neither a test nor another drill. This was real, and he was about to travel not only through space but into what they were quite certain was another galaxy altogether.

Every show, movie, and book he'd ever encountered about such travels began to play back in his mind. Some snippets he could piece together—travels to places that had pyramids like in Egypt, ancient races, and even Atlantis. He doubted very much that he'd experience anything like that, but the reality that awaited him had the prospect of being way more exciting.

Voices started going off in his comms as they turned on the systems in preparation for a smooth departure. There were systems checks and the colonel was making some joke about conquering the universe, but Trent was focused on his heavy breathing and the way his left pectoral was twitching as sometimes happened in moments of excitement, not to mention the vision above. Part of him said to turn back, run away. An image flashed through his mind of going through the gate, only to come out the other side with his skin turned inside out and his organs floating through space. But the rational side of him told those fears to shut up. He was going to be a hero, one of the first humans ever to cross to the other side. If they were lucky, they'd even be the team that first stepped foot on the planet that would be home to humanity's first colony.

Only a few paces away, the ship doors opened automatically. He glanced back to see the other teams coming behind—six in all for six ships. Each ship would take approximately two dozen, including flight crews, infantry, and botanists. They sure looked grand, these Space Fleet Marines in their body armor of grayish blue with red visors. Most had their visors up, but others had lowered them, really getting into their roles. It gave him the feeling of a VR first-person shooter. Only, this wasn't a game; this was reality.

With a deep breath, he turned to continue onto his ship, then froze. He looked again to make sure that what he'd seen wasn't just a trick of the light, but it wasn't. Shapes were moving just out of view in the shadows. Fast. They charged in, and then they were fully visible—men and women in similar uniforms as his own, some of them. No, not quite. They weren't in Space Fleet Marine armor, but they were wearing uniforms—exoskeletons—and some had chest guards and other layers of body armor.

His own genetic modifications made him fast, but not as fast as these people.

"What the hell is that?" one of the voices said into his comms as guards charged out, shouting for the newcomers to halt.

Another voice shouted, "Into the ships, now!"

Trent turned, running to obey orders even as he heard a scream from the tail end of the group. He looked and saw that the strangers had taken down one of the Marines. That moment it took to see this and debate going back for them was enough for two more strangers to catch him. They had appeared from the shadows to his left, meaning they likely had all directions covered.

Whatever the hell this was, he wasn't going down without a fight. Even as he saw their red, glowing eyes, he was dodging, pulling out his Ka-Bar knife with one hand and his blaster pistol with his other. He had taken both opponents down before he saw a third leaping for him.

It took him, snarling. This woman had red, glowing eyes like the others, and veins popped from her neck and forehead. Her skin looked slightly scaly, like she was suffering from some sort of disease or outbreak. She was struggling against him, teeth snapping as if she was trying to bite his face off.

A punch landed upside her head and then another, followed by a blaster shot that left her in a heap of smoking ruin. Something moved at his right and he saw a shadow. Turning to attack, he stopped with his pistol aimed at the colonel's forehead.

"In your ship, Marine!" Colonel O'Donnell shouted, grabbing him and shoving him toward the open door.

He ran, seeing other strangers coming at her. But she was fast, and soon she was with him, charging through. Together, they managed to secure the doors before the attackers could reach them.

"Get us in the air!" Colonel O'Donnell yelled, and she pulled Trent with her, shoving him into his seat before going to her own and strapping in. "Skip checks. Just do it!"

Trent sat there, listening to the banging and pounding from outside. He heard a new round of gunfire and blasts, and then the ship was moving. They were out of there, and he could finally sit back and try to calm his nerves. Adrenaline pushed him, making him want to stand and fight, to run back down there and kill those bastards.

But it was over. The ship was in the air, leaving that problem for someone else to deal with. All that mattered now was that soon he'd be through the gate.

2

SHRINA: EARTH, WASHINGTON, D.C

Everyone gathered in the room at the W Hotel was top of the shelf as far as Washington politics, and somehow Shrina Collins was there among them, unable to believe her luck. It wasn't that she didn't understand why she was there. She had, after all, been involved in a major operation to save the President of the United States. She had also proven herself in a raid in Dubai that had arguably played a large role in the downfall of the corporation known as New Origins, therefore making the U.S. military's super-soldier program possible. But that didn't mean she felt comfortable there. She'd almost rather be back home with her little sister, Prestige, watching the launch with her, although there was certainly something to be said for schmoozing with these people while watching from the large screen along the wall, everyone cheering as the early preparations began.

After it started, she'd gone off to find a drink and been cornered by a man she hadn't thought she'd see again in quite some time.

"Secretary Veles," she said, nodding to the man next to her.

He held two drinks and handed her one. "Saw you over here, grabbed you a drink. Alicia's sister, right?"

They'd met only once when the president had briefly introduced them. It wasn't like the president really knew Shrina either, and he'd given more credit for the success of the operation to Alicia and Marick—her sister and her sister's husband. Still, he'd made the introduction, and the secretary had been overly excited, claiming he was close to both Alicia and Marick, and had played his part in taking down New Origins.

He knew very well who she was. She smiled, accepting the drink.

"The SIG is treating you well? I don't think we've had the chance to speak since you were accepted, and I wanted to congratulate you."

"Thank you, sir." The Shared Intelligence Group had been her dream back then when she was with the FBI and looking for advancement. Now she was in, though still quite junior. "I'm learning, adapting."

"I'm sure you are." Veles took a sip and winked. "My nephew is here, by the way." He pointed to a man with broad shoulders and curly hair cropped fairly short. The man wasn't bad to look at, but she wasn't there to be set up with anyone.

"He must be smart," she said, smiling at the implied compliment.

"What? Married now, like Alicia?" His smile faltered. "I don't suppose you've heard from her."

"Not a peep, and no to the married thing, too," Shrina admitted. For the first two years she'd been in contact with her sister, and then… nothing. After checking in and following up via the business card Veles had given her, she'd found out it was the same with the others. Nobody had heard from anyone who'd escaped the day New Origins fell.

She'd gone through a worried phase, knowing Alicia and her husband had been experimented on with the same method used to genetically modify these new super soldiers. But as she watched the new program develop, she knew it couldn't have been used on them. Or she hoped. There was still a chance the previous test subjects, including her sister, had received a less evolved version of the modifications.

That conversation had been the last time she and Veles had spoken, and she'd had no updates since.

Veles seemed lost in thought, staring over his drink at the view of the White House and the National Monument—both enhanced versions of what they'd once been. The White House had been built up like a fortress, a necessary evolution considering the various attacks over the last hundred years, and the monument served as a defensive tower now. It was quite the sight to behold—a symbol among the old relics of D.C. and a reminder of what the city had grown into.

"Sir," she said, and then cleared her throat. "Sir?"

He turned toward her with a smile but then frowned, glancing over his shoulder as a commotion rose in the crowd. Not only in the crowd, Shrina saw, but on the screen. Her hands felt suddenly clammy and her drink nearly slipped out of her grasp, but she caught it with her other hand and stood, holding it with both and watching with wide eyes.

The reporter was saying there had been a problem, while the feeds showed figures darting out from the darkness around the launch, attacking the Marines. It was like they were trying to take over the spacecraft, she thought, and then some of them actually had.

"Holy shit!" Veles said, glancing her way with a compassionate look. "Isn't…"

"Trent," she said, nodding, not able to finish the sentence. Her ex—the man she'd gone through so much with. They'd only split up so they could each pursue their careers, and now he was one of those Marines being attacked. He had wanted to join the Space Fleet Marines so he could go through the gateway to the stars when the time came. Shrina couldn't be the one at home always wondering what he was up to or worried that something would go wrong. Unfortunately, that choice hadn't done anything to stop her from filling with dread at this sight.

Screams carried out from the feed, and then one of the ships took off with another behind it, shooting it down. Her hands went to her mouth, the glass falling and shattering at her feet. Others had similar reactions, and already the Secret Service was moving the president out of there as sirens sounded in the distance.

She assumed they were moving in to help get him to safety, but then she heard screaming in the streets. The commotion wasn't just coming from the screen! Spinning, she darted for the balcony, hitting her hip against the food table on the way and knocking over a tray of deviled eggs. When she reached the balcony railing, she looked down to see total chaos—figures were advancing, mostly sticking to the shadows, and attacking people.

A glance back at the feed showed more cities, more attacks, and then an emergency warning went up. It cut out the news and told everyone to get inside and remain calm while authorities dealt with the situation.

"What the hell's happening?" she said, turning to see Veles being escorted out. He saw her, pulled on the agent with him, and gestured her way. There was an argument, but Veles shoved the guy and ran to her.

"You're with us! Move!"

She didn't argue, and the agent was already back into his role, glaring but doing what he needed to do to try and protect the secretary.

They headed for the stairs, descending as quickly as the group could move, and the agents led them to the waiting cars. Some of the agents then moved out into the street to take up a defensive position. The secretary was already in the car that had been specified for his use when a red-eyed man appeared, moving faster than the agents could react. He had a rifle and shot two of the agents, then slammed another one onto the ground between Shrina and the car.

Forget that. She took off, cursing herself for wearing heels. She tore them off, running with one in each hand, and darted across Lafayette Square. As she moved toward the north end of the park, she pulled up her wrist computer and dialed Prestige. No luck—the signals weren't getting through. Everyone was likely trying to make calls. Or worse, the attackers had somehow jammed the signals.

She reached H Street and turned left, the pavement tearing at her feet. A dad ran by with a small boy in his arms, likely out to watch the historic take-off, and now their lives were at risk. More screams echoed throughout the capital, and more people were running.

One of the attackers leaped out to attack the dad, and Shrina didn't even think twice. She jumped, pulled back, and thrust the heel of her shoe into the attacker's skull. He turned to her, red eyes fading, and collapsed.

"Damn," the dad said, then added, "thank you," before retreating down a stairway to hide out in one of the local bars.

Shrina stood there, staring at the dead man. There didn't seem to be anything unusual about him, aside from those dead red eyes that now stared back at her, but she wasn't sure. She knelt, glancing around to be sure she wasn't in immediate danger, then stared at the man. His teeth looked sharper than normal and longer too. Not a *vampire,* she thought. No, of course there weren't vampires!

But there was no doubt that this man had red eyes and that his teeth were abnormal. Genetic modifications of some sort? Knowing that they'd given the super soldiers of New Origins and the Space Fleet Marines increased strength, speed, and even an enhanced ability to heal, she could see how something could be done in a similar fashion to create these monsters.

Maybe.

Sticking around and debating with herself wasn't going to keep her alive long enough to get answers, though. She sprinted off, but when she turned the corner up Connecticut Avenue toward the trains, she saw a group of the attackers moving her way. Cops were firing at them with no luck.

She decided in that moment that no matter what it took, she needed to get home to check on Prestige and their grandparents. If the trains weren't an option, she'd have to find a plan B, which quickly materialized in the form of one of the police pods, floating a few feet back from the cops with its door ajar. They were likely freaking out, leading to them being careless.

She hated that she was doing it but saw no other

way. Charging forward, she reached the pod as the attackers reached the police, one of them taking the closest cop down. If she'd had enhancements, or a weapon, or even shoes she could run in, she would've stayed to fight. But she didn't have any of that, and her little sister needed her. The rest of the cops fell as Shrina threw the pod into drive and hightailed it out of there.

The city was falling, she thought with horror. Earlier that day she'd been worried about the threat from space when it was—as it had always been—right here on Earth. She tried to call her family as she drove, hitting her wrist device when it wouldn't connect.

Hang in there, Prestige, she thought. *I'll be there soon.*

3

TRENT: SPACE, EN ROUTE TO THE GATE

"We've got a problem," Colonel O'Donnell said, moving back from the cockpit where she'd gone to check in with the pilot.

"What's happening out there?" one of the other Marines asked.

"Those assailants took over two of the ships and shot down one of ours," she said, her expression grim. No more jokes from her, not at a time like this.

"Let me guess," Trent said. "We have no idea who the enemy is."

She shook her head. "Comms from the ground have stopped, but the last we heard was more screaming and shouting. Whoever it is might have taken over down there, or is at least leading an attack that will have us out of commission for the foreseeable future. Rather, *they'll* be out of commission. We're still going full steam ahead."

"We're going through the gate?" Trent asked, worried they would've cancelled the mission if communication with mission command went out.

"If we're not shot down first," the colonel said, strapping in again. "And that brings me to my next point. Hold the hell on."

As she said it, the ship was already turning and a new round of turret shots could be heard and felt, vibrating through the ship.

"We're engaging," she said. "Our main goal is to get as many friendly ships through as we can, ASAP."

"Let's just hope we don't shoot down the wrong one," another Marine said, and Trent grunted. A very real concern.

"Colonel," the pilot called through the system's comms, "another of ours is down. Two left, but we're almost to the gate."

"Chances of getting shot down before we make it?" the colonel asked through her comms.

"Looking less likely, but the other ship is ahead, sir."

"Punch it," the colonel said.

"Roger that."

The Marines were pushed back in their seats, all of them feeling the rattling. Trent's stomach churned as his last dinner threatened to come up. A Marine was actually whimpering at his side, though he couldn't turn to see who it was and, frankly, didn't want to know.

His own fear was threatening to take over, but he focused, watching through the cockpit window to see the gate as it rose up around them. It was large enough for two or three of their ships at a time, no more.

CRASH!

"Contact!" the pilot shouted, and then they saw another ship—the one that had presumably hit them—fly off through the gate. A second later, the purple and blue light enveloped them and, as emergency lights flashed and the pilot shouted about various functions not responding, they were whisked away, the light flashing and blinding…

…and then they were through.

All was calm and the light faded.

Trent leaned back, staring out at a section of space no other human had ever beheld. This wasn't likely anywhere near their solar system. For all he knew, it could be on the other side of the universe, as far as one could possibly go within comprehension, or even farther than that. A Marine to his left let out a shout of excitement, and then Ellins was saying that they'd made it, that they were through.

All he could do was breathe, trying to push back the emotions that welled up in him. This was a dream several years in the making—one that had now come true.

He was among the first humans to ever go through a real gateway to the stars. He closed his eyes, imagining the look of pride on his dad's face if he knew Trent had made it through. But as far as everyone on Earth knew, Trent was dead after the attack.

That could still very well turn out to be the case if he gave up. This wasn't the end of him, though. He'd show them all. None of his worries and none of his nostalgic bull mattered anymore. Nothing else mattered but this moment. He opened his eyes and smiled across at the colonel.

Her eyes moved to the display, her face contorting to an expression of terror. He frowned, wondering what could cause that emotion in the woman, and turned to get a look.

At first, he encountered nothing but empty space. Then he saw them—huge, red eyes that seemed to drift through space... coming right for them.

Everyone froze, the chaos and excitement from moments before no longer important. A voice broke through the comms—Sergeant Espinoza, who was on one of the ships Enise wasn't on. Trent's heart broke at the thought that she might already be gone. That sorrow was stronger than the fear he felt at seeing those large, red eyes, so he was the first on his ship to snap out of it. Attacks were coming from all directions, though they couldn't see from what. Screams took over the comms, but Trent was focused on survival.

"Colonel!" he shouted, but got only a blank stare. He undid his harness and threw himself at her, grabbing her shoulders and shouting again, "Colonel O'Donnell, get us out of here!"

She turned to him, blinked, and then seemed to wake from a distant dream. In an instant she was shouting commands, and the pilot was maneuvering and attempting to fire back while shouting about not knowing where to shoot. A ship appeared before them, a moment later being struck and shattered into pieces.

Comms were flooded with distress calls. Marines, trained for combat, were screaming like children. Then those red, glowing eyes appeared again at the same time that one last ship registered on the display and the gate closed.

Trent turned to the display, watching the ship approach and wondering which side it was on. Could Enise be on that ship, or was it the sons of bitches who'd attacked them? He held out hope, but it was a hope that didn't last long as his ship began to shake and a bright light tore through it. He slammed down his faceplate, already helping others unhitch themselves as the ship started to fall apart.

He turned and ran, going all out for the escape pods and shouting for the others to do the same. Throwing himself in, the pod closed but allowed him a quick glimpse. The others weren't going to make it in time! Bits of the ship were already breaking off, and a figure he saw running toward him was pulled out into space. Trent tried to escape the automatic straps, but it was too late.

"Colonel!" he shouted into his comms. "Anyone? Who else made it to the pods?!"

No answer.

Before he even had a chance to think of options, the pod thrust out into space with a jolt, and he watched as his ship was no more. All of the colonel's aspirations were gone, just like that. Those young Marines who had simply hoped to see space and be part of something big were all gone, too. When all he could see was space as his pod spun and the automatic navigation took control, his fear overcame him. Red blotched his vision and his breathing seemed uncontrollable.

It was all falling apart. As far as he knew, he was stranded in another galaxy… alone.

4

ESPINOZA: SPACE, KRASTION GALAXY

Espinoza's ship had been in the lead when the shots hit. Nobody knew where the attack was coming from or what was happening, and he couldn't stop shouting into the damn comms. It wasn't that he thought it would do any good—they'd just gone through the gateway into another galaxy, their ship spiraling out of control from the hit they'd taken. And there he was, shouting, "Mayday! Get us some damn help! Mayday!"

Others with him were silent. Gunnery Sergeant Ellins was at his side, staring at him intently, as if letting her eyes leave his would mean death. And in a way, it calmed him. The ship was hurtling into nothingness, all the other ships having been blown up, and those gray eyes were taking him out of there.

"We're dead anyway," Ellins said. She leaned in

and grabbed him by the metal of his collar, pulling him in and pressing her lips to his.

When she pulled back, she continued to stare into his eyes until the pilot caught their attention, shouting, "Planet! We have the planet!"

"What?" Ellins said, turning toward the pilot and releasing Espinoza.

"Like I said," the pilot shouted, "we're coming in hot, but the planet's right there."

"Can you land us?" Ellins asked.

"It's that or die, so I'm gonna try my damnedest."

Another ship hurtled by in the distance, then disappeared from view, and Espinoza's team was in full-on pull-themselves-out-of-panic mode. While the others might all be gone, they still had a shot, it seemed.

"Get Earth on comms!" Ellins commanded. "If there's any way to get a signal, I want it done!"

"Roger that," Espinoza said, still trying to process what had happened with the kiss. His holoscreen showed no signal, but he tried anyway. He then attempted to relay it off of the other ships as he'd been taught, but no luck. It wasn't as if they didn't have a signal out there. It was more likely something had broken off during the shooting. He ran a diagnostic and cursed.

"What is it?" Ellins asked.

"Half the system seems to be knocked out," he said. "And by that, I mean out of the ship. Gone during the fighting."

"Meaning we're stranded until they send more ships to find us, if they do."

He nodded. "Or... until we find the right materials on this planet to rebuild it."

"That's a big if," she said.

"Everyone hold on!" the pilot shouted, and then they were shaking. Orange and red flashed outside the windows, and the display at the front of the ship showed images of the planet below as it searched for the prime place to land. It was hopeful, as the images showed several bodies of water, vegetation, and hills.

BAM! The ship jerked and began spiraling violently out of control. The back half tore off, taking Corporal Brown with it. The man reached, eyes wide, and then was gone. Sky spun around them, and then the emergency thrusters kicked in, but nearly too late. The ship shuddered and crashed. There was a ringing and then blackness, and then Espinoza was out.

As he came to, Espinoza realized he couldn't have been out for long because blood was still fresh on Kim's forehead. She sat toward the front, limp. Smoke was rising from the ship, and Espinoza realized he needed to get out of there. Quickly undoing his harness, he checked for other survivors. Ellins was on the ground, recovering and alive. He pulled her up and they looked for the pilot, Captain Thomas. There was no sign of him there, but when they spotted the back half of the ship and made their way to it, they found him on the red sand, crawling away from the ship. Corporal Brown appeared a moment later, staggering toward them.

"You... made it?" Espinoza asked.

Brown grunted, staggered, but caught himself.

"Check on Kim," Ellins said, grabbing the med kits and a pack of food while Espinoza followed her orders.

Others from the crew were already moving out, scattering in a state of disorientation. He passed them, nodding and asking if they were okay. Many simply staggered on, but a couple of them asked where they were needed. A young corporal named Franco turned and joined him, and they went back to where he'd found Kim. She was pinned down and her leg was stuck but not bleeding or looking like it had been crushed.

"Help me push," Espinoza said, getting into position with his back against the floor and his feet on the metal dash that was holding her in.

Kim's eyes had a distant look to them, like she

was waking from a deep sleep. When she saw them helping, she muttered, "Thank God."

"Don't forget to thank *us* while you're at it," Franco said, taking up a position beside Espinoza.

"Of course."

"She still didn't say it," Franco whispered.

Espinoza ignored him and said, "Push!" Together they heaved, but the metal only budged slightly.

"We're going to need more Marines," Franco said.

"Or..." Espinoza knew it was risky, but he had to try. "Since this thing could blow at any moment, how about we get her the hell out of here?"

"Tell me you have a plan, and I'm in."

"Thrusters." Espinoza positioned himself again, this time making sure to angle his feet away from Kim.

"You're nuts." Franco moved away from him and pulled up his faceplate. "What if it fries us? Or cripples our legs, like that?"

"We're strong. We have the exoskeletons built into the suits." Espinoza motioned for him to get down. "Join me."

Franco cursed and glanced over at Kim, who shrugged. "Fine, but if we die, I'm dragging you down to hell with me no matter what Peter says, or whoever's supposed to be at the gates."

"Deal." Espinoza turned to Kim. "Brace yourself,

it might get hot. And when you feel like you can move, get out of there."

"You don't have to tell me twice," she replied and turned, brow furrowed as she focused on the moment. At the last minute, she closed her faceplate and Franco was smart enough to do the same.

"Three, two, go!" Espinoza pushed with his thrusters, legs pressed against the caved-in metal, and felt his back taking a lot of the pressure as he was pressed to the floor. Franco's thrusters were going too, and readings on the HUD screen showed it was getting hot. Thrusters were meant for outdoors—to slow a fall from great heights—not this.

Yet, the plan was working. In a matter of seconds, Kim was out, rolling away from them to safety, and Franco cut off his thrusters. That left Espinoza with too much weight to hold up, so the metal fell back in place with a crunch and sent a wave of pain through Espinoza. His muscles cramped and he grunted.

He was enhanced, though. He'd heal.

"Get out," he told them, already rolling and starting to move, taking it slowly as his body worked out the stiffness. The other two were out first and then him, all of them charging for the group of Marines who had gathered around the gunny and the captain.

First there was a small explosion, one that simply startled Espinoza and his two companions, but the next was large enough to send them staggering. He lost his footing and fell but was helped up by Kim a moment later as Franco kept on moving. After two steps, the man looked back and saw that they were dragging, so he came to help.

"All good?" he asked, but Espinoza waved him on.

"Way to go, Marines," Gunny said, joining them but then ducking as another explosion rocked the ship and sent debris flying. A chunk of metal landed in a tree next to them, but others pounded off of the Marines' armor. Thankfully, no one was hurt.

For the first time, Espinoza noticed the trees—short, like a cross between a palm and a tulip, with large leaves that reached up and curled in. They were strange plants, but plants nonetheless. A more focused glance around showed him that there was other vegetation, though sparse.

Turning back to watch the smoke rise up into the sky with the others, Espinoza shook his head. "Too bad Earth can't see that. We could send smoke signals."

Ellins glared at him.

"You know, like Native Americans," Espinoza said, motioning with his hands. "Smoke signals?"

"No, I got it," she replied, then walked off to give

orders to the others about getting the fire under control.

"I thought for sure we were dead meat," Kim said, running her hands across her armor to check for holes or missing limbs. "I'm still not totally sure I'm in one piece, or that this is real."

"Your leg okay?" Espinoza asked.

She moved it, rotating it at the joint, and nodded. "This isn't the worst I've been through."

"No?"

"Once, I was at a movie theater and they had no Sour Patch Kids," she said, deadpan. "Now *that* was a tough day."

Franco chuckled. "Yeah, I hear that. Once I had a female roommate who could never remember to leave the seat up when she was done with the toilet. The worst, every single day."

"I think you two don't quite get what's actually happening here," Espinoza said with a roll of his eyes.

"Relax," Kim said. "Just trying to figure out how to not freak the hell out right now and go running off a cliff in panic mode. I mean… on the comms, they were calling them vampires. Then there was something else attacking us when we came through…"

"Yeah, what was that?" Franco asked, his smile gone now.

"I think the better question is," Espinoza said, "will they be coming after us?"

"Damn." Franco shook his head. "I hadn't even thought of it like that."

Kim apparently hadn't either because she was looking at the sky with horror. It was enough to make him want to play their game and get their minds off the subject.

"Worst for me..." Espinoza said, appearing very thoughtful. "Oh, one time on a bus full of kids—I think it was sixth grade—I had to take a piss really bad. We couldn't find a bathroom—"

"You pissed yourself?" Franco said with a grin.

"No, but they let me off finally, right there on the road. Everyone was cheering me on while I pissed, and it was so embarrassing. No stage fright, at least, but then this gust of wind hits—"

"Oh no," Kim said.

"Yeah, a good spray all across my pants. So the rest of the ride, I'm not only the guy everyone cheered on while peeing; I'm the guy with a line of it going down my pants leg. It dried up of course, but still."

"Hey, too bad the wind didn't splash it all over

those kids," Kim said. "That would've been a good story."

Espinoza grinned, glad to have helped take the focus off the grief of losing others and the terror of possibly being attacked at any minute.

Many of the Marines had their faceplates up, and Ellins explained that they'd get additional tests on air and soil going as soon as everyone was settled. Since they hadn't really been given the option to proceed with caution, they were damn glad the drone's results from earlier expeditions had been accurate about the planet having breathable air.

When they were sure the ship had finished with its temper tantrum, they sent in a crew to put out the remaining fires and Kim went back in to see about getting comms up.

Sunset came soon after, a strange ordeal on an alien planet. The clouds were more like threads in the sky, the sunset tinged with florescent green and bright red as if the Northern lights back on Earth had been strewn with rivers of blood. Cold gusts of wind hit them, so many of the Marines put their faceplates back up.

Captain Thomas started a fire, thinking logically that anything that could see them would've already seen them because of the explosions and resulting smoke, so a fire for warmth seemed warranted.

Some of the Marines removed their armor, getting comfortable in their body-tight uniforms, while Gunny set up a system of patrols and outposts to ensure the group's safety.

Some of them argued for moving away from the crash site, but they didn't yet know if the planet supported intelligent life. Their only hope of returning to Earth seemed to lie with Kim figuring out how to get the comms working again, so they stayed close to the ship.

"What in the name of all that's holy happened up there?" Franco asked as he and Espinoza returned from a patrol.

"Or back on Earth," Espinoza replied, though his focus was elsewhere. His eyes were drawn to those of the gunny as she sat by the fire, staring into the flames.

"They've likely cleared that up by now," Franco said. "They'll probably have new ships up and through the gate in no time."

"Even then, how would they find us? The ship's down, comms too. They'd have to fly over the whole planet, searching."

"Damn," Franco said, slipping out of his armor to join the others at the fire. "Talk about a downer."

Espinoza mumbled an apology and then excused himself, finding a seat next to the gunny.

"I told my mom this was going to change lives," someone was saying on the other side of her, talking to a couple of the other Marines. "Shit… I didn't know that just meant it'd ruin ours."

"Game's not over," one of them replied. "And I still got a pocket full of quarters."

"What the hell's that mean?"

"Just… don't you read history?" the guy said with a laugh. "Come on, back in the day? Machines with games? Quarters?"

Nothing.

Espinoza had to chuckle. He was almost tempted to pull up one of the hologames from his wrist piece, but instead he pulled up his courage to do what he'd come there for. Eyeing Ellins, he went for it.

"Gunny," he whispered, leaning in so only she could hear him. "About what happened back there…"

She turned to him, eyes firm. "Nothing happened, Sergeant."

He frowned, unable to block that kiss from his mind. His adrenaline had been rushing and he had feared for his life, but the kiss had taken over and now it was there to stay. When she looked away again, he saw something in her eyes as the reflection of the fire caught them—she was conflicted.

It was enough to know that, for now.

Some of the others were ready to try and get some sleep, but not Espinoza. He volunteered for first watch. It was eerie, finding himself the only one from his team awake on this planet. For all he knew, he was the only one awake at all on this planet, but he had a feeling that wouldn't be the case.

All around, hills and trees formed silhouettes in the night. For a moment, he could almost believe he was back home. He could almost trick himself into thinking this was just another night, and that in the morning he'd go find somewhere to eat waffles with extra helpings of whipped cream—his go-to comfort food whenever he returned from a deployment. It had also worked as his standard way of dealing with a hangover, he remembered with a chuckle. One an ex-girlfriend had taught him, the same one who had offered to fool around the night before he left for the star gate. Now, not knowing when any of that would happen again, he wondered if he had made the wrong choice by turning her down.

Something pulled at his nerves, and he was reminded where he was—standing alone on an alien planet with only these sleeping Marines around him. He wouldn't have traded them for anyone else, though. He glanced over and allowed his eyes to linger on the gunny. She was attractive with her auburn hair pulled back into a ponytail and light freckles across her nose. Fraternization was a big deal in the Marines, so he got why she was acting withdrawn. But if they were truly stuck up there, stranded, maybe to die… he didn't give a damn about fraternization rules.

Something moved in the shadows over by the far hill. He took a deep breath, lowering his helmet and faceplate. The HUD screen on his faceplate confirmed that there was something out there, but as fast as it had shown up on the screen, it was gone. If he hadn't seen it himself, he might have thought it was a malfunction.

His first reaction was to go to the captain, but he was injured. The man needed his rest.

"Gunny," Espinoza said, nudging her gently, "we're not alone."

She rubbed her eyes and licked her lips as she looked up at him, then sat up. "What? I told you, it was nothing. Even if we *are* alone…"

"No, gunny. I said we're *not* alone." He leaned back, too worried to be annoyed at her rebuff. "I saw movement. My HUD confirmed it."

At those words she was fully alert and standing, pulling on her own helmet to check the HUD. "Where?"

Espinoza indicated the hill where he'd seen it.

"Whatever's out there, it's fast. As quick as I scanned it, the thing ran off."

She nodded, grabbed a rifle and nodded at his. "Locked and loaded?"

He grinned. "Always. Oh, you mean the rifle?"

"Sergeant…" She looked around at the other sleeping Marines and shook her head. "I shouldn't have done it, okay? Kissing you was—"

"Don't say it," Espinoza said, holding up a hand. "I got it. But if we find out we're not getting out of this, maybe you ignore protocol?"

She hesitated, glanced back out at the hill, and said, "Maybe."

They took the watches in pairs from then on, though Espinoza was pretty sure the rest experienced a sleep as restless as his, knowing they weren't alone.

5

SHRINA: EARTH, VIRGINIA

Shrina flew the pod over the tall apartment buildings where she still lived with her younger sister, Prestige, and their grandparents. It wasn't far from the Pentagon Row shopping center, and the lights from that direction lit up the sky in an orange haze. Breaking a moment that could have almost felt peaceful, an explosion from the direction of the Pentagon went off in the distance, along with gunshots. It was at times like these that she wished she lived far away from anything related to the government.

How many of these genetically modified creatures could there be, to be attacking like this? Cars were driving away from the city, and several pods were flying out as well. (Pods were still mostly limited to the authorities and the wealthy.) She was able to land in the yard outside her apartment building and immediately dialed her sister again.

"Hello?" the girl said in a hushed voice.

"Prestige?" Shrina's lip quivered at the sound of her sister's voice. At least she was alive and presumably safe. "I'm coming up. Don't go anywhere."

"I'm not at home."

All of that relief flooded out of Shrina as she began to imagine worst-case scenarios. "Where are you?"

"I went over to the clubhouse to watch," Prestige said. "A couple of the vampires were spotted and everyone ran, so—"

"Vampires?"

"Those things… red eyes, fangs."

"Dear, they aren't vampires," Shrina assured her. "As scary as it is, I can promise that."

"Well, that's what all the newsfeeds are calling them. So yeah. There you go."

Shrina frowned, circling around toward the center of the buildings. "You're at the clubhouse?"

"We ran… got stuck in a parking garage."

Shrina cursed and aimed the pod down, searching for signs of a parking garage near the clubhouse. It didn't make sense to her that these bastards were attacking out here in the apartments—areas that had no value. If they were terrorists, she supposed it *could* make sense to cause random fear and havoc in places that wouldn't otherwise make sense. Whatever this was, it certainly wasn't a regular terrorist attack. She'd seen the space launch interruption on the screen and could tell the attackers had been trained—likely former military and genetically modified to boot. Nothing here seemed to be harmed, however, so it was possible the ones who'd come through here were on their way to the Pentagon or elsewhere in the city to join forces with other groups.

"Okay, I see the parking garage," Shrina said and landed nearby. "Come on out."

"I want to," Prestige said, voice uncertain, "but… I think there's one of those things here."

"What?"

"I saw it… red, glowing eyes."

Shrina couldn't wrap her mind around what one of them would be doing here, not unless this was all random. With a sigh, she turned back to the police pod and grabbed the only weapon still inside—an arc baton, one of the kinds that shot electricity from the tip.

It would have to do.

"Where are you in the parking garage?" Shrina asked.

No answer came. She frowned and jogged over

to the parking garage, eyes searching the shadows for any sort of lurking vampires or whatever they were. She rolled her eyes at herself but figured that if everyone else was calling them vampires, it wouldn't hurt for her to go with it.

"Down the stairs," Prestige whispered. "Careful, I think he's near the top, or in the stairwell."

Great.

Shrina moved toward the stairs, wishing it wasn't so damned dark in there. You'd think that, since the world had been able to expand into space and terraform planets, they'd at least be able to put lights in a damn parking lot.

Her hands were shaking, her head spinning. She wasn't going to deny that she was scared, but that didn't mean anything here. If she let her sister get hurt, she wouldn't be able to forgive herself. Prestige had been a neighbor once, before her parents died in the last war. Since Shrina's grandparents had adopted Shrina and Alicia after their parent's deaths, they then also adopted Prestige. While Shrina's career meant she didn't get to see her grandparents or Prestige very often, she one-hundred percent considered Prestige a true sister—one for whom she would do anything.

A clanking sound came from her left. It could just be the pipes or a rat, she told herself. It *could* be, but knowing her luck, it wasn't. Each step she took was cautious, and she was careful not to make a sound. She moved to a van along the wall, going behind it and pausing, listening.

"Shrina?" Prestige whispered again. "I'm… I mean, are you coming?"

"One second," Shrina replied, and then a figure dashed out. Damn. Damn! She backed up, rod at the ready, but she heard a whimper from the stairway and so did the figure. It turned from her and crashed through the door to the stairs.

Her sister was down there and was likely the one whose whimper had drawn the vampire. Shrina wasn't about to let that happen so she jumped up, kicking off of the wall to leap over the front of the van, and dove into the stairwell.

There was someone there all right, but it wasn't her sister, and Shrina was too late. A woman, older than Shrina by about ten years, collapsed as the vampire moved for the door beyond.

It turned to see Shrina, and she could tell that it was a man, or once had been. He was Asian, with the muscles of a fighter, and he paused between her and Prestige's shouts when she saw her older sister. Before the son of a bitch could make up his mind, however, Shrina had thrown herself down the stairs, jumping from the rail and bringing her arc rod around to slam into the vampire's chest. He went flying back and crashed into the car beyond. Glass shattered and metal caved, and the vampire fell limp.

Shrina's nerves were on edge, so when another shadow moved she was prepared for anything, turning for the attack. But it was only her sister. Prestige had her frizzy black hair tied back, and her wide eyes were staring at her older sister with confusion. Shrina always dressed as if she were going out on the town, and that night was no exception.

"How...?" Prestige asked, turning to see the damage.

Without answering, Shrina darted forward and took hold of her sister, gripping her in a tight embrace. Finally, she pulled back and said, "We have to go! Now!"

Prestige didn't argue, but as soon as they turned to go, another vampire appeared. He was a hulking beast of a man, twice as big as the last, and his eyes glowed red but he seemed confused. He growled and clawed at the air, then turned and stumbled about.

When he stopped, sniffed the air, and then turned toward them, Shrina wasn't sure if she should be afraid or feel pity for the thing. Still, she had her sister to worry about, so as the vampire came at her with incredible speed, she brought the arc baton up and drove a bolt of electricity into him that sent him flying away. The force sent her sprawling, too, but Prestige was at her side, helping her stand.

The vampire was up now, but he was just staring at them as the redness faded from his eyes. He reached out, desperate. "It's you… run! Hide!"

As little sense as that made coming from him, they did as he advised. Without a backward glance, they were soon out of the parking garage and into the pod. Two thuds sounded and Prestige shrieked. A glance back showed two new vampires had just slammed into the pod, one twice as thick as most men. His muscles bulged and his eyes flared as he came at them, slamming both fists into the glass and creating a small crack.

When he pulled back again, Shrina reached out and grabbed Prestige's hand. The glass cracked again, part of it falling in and creating a hole the size of a baseball.

"You won't make it far," the vampire snarled, face close to the hole. "We *will* find you."

Shrina released her sister's hand, snatched up her arc rod, and jammed it through the hole so that the electricity flared when it made contact with the vampire's eye. He shot back, screaming and growling, and before the other could react or the first could recover, Shrina took off, rising up into the sky. Another thud sounded and the pod shook, but they didn't stop. As they flew off, they caught a glimpse of the previous vampire staggering off, the other two staring up at them.

"We're getting you home," Shrina said.

"They... they knew you," Prestige said and turned to assess her sister. "Why?"

"I have no clue," Shrina admitted. "But we need to get you, Poppa, and Grams out of here."

"They weren't answering," Prestige said, voice growing silent.

"I'm sure they're fine."

Prestige didn't look convinced but sat back in her seat, letting it go. If these vampires were really looking for Shrina, it was possible they'd found out where she lived, but that still didn't make any sense.

After a moment, Prestige said, "Are we in a police pod?"

Shrina bit her lip and shrugged. "Yes."

"I'm going to assume the FBI lets you have these..."

"No." They flew in silence for a moment before she added, "And I'm not exactly with the FBI anymore. Kind of, but I'm on assignment with the SIG."

"Oh, damn." Prestige laughed. "But that still doesn't explain why you have a police pod."

"I stole it to get to you."

Prestige grinned. "That's the sis I remember. Not this FBI lady."

"SIG," Shrina corrected her, but she couldn't help smiling. "I'll have time to teach you the intricacies of that later, but right now we need to check on the apartment."

Prestige's face went pale, but Shrina was busy lowering the pod to the rooftop. She wasn't going to take chances, and since the apartment was on the fourteenth flour, this made the most sense.

"Stay in the pod. Lock it," she said, finalizing the landing. "Don't open the doors for anyone but me."

Shooting sounded in the distance and military pods and choppers flew through the sky. Apparently, the fighting was far from over.

"What then?" Prestige asked.

"We find you somewhere safe," Shrina said as her mind went to Trent. She was worried about him, wondering if he'd somehow made it and if the attackers had, too. They couldn't all be mindless or they wouldn't have been able to fly. Yet, the second attacker they'd encountered in the parking garage had certainly seemed out of it—more like a man on drugs than a vampire.

The real reason her mind had gone to Trent, though, was that he'd looked her up once when he was in town and they'd hung out, talking about the crazy times they'd experienced together. He'd been driving and had to stop by his dad's place in Bethesda, Maryland. It wasn't so far, and the old man had taken a liking to Shrina because she'd complimented the gun collection he'd felt compelled to show off. Even though she didn't know him very well, it was worth a shot to go there and hide out. He was likely worried about his boy and could use the company.

"I've got something in mind," she said, motioning for Prestige to stay put.

The night was otherwise calm, if one could ignore the shooting and explosions in the distance. It was as if the city on one side of the apartments was experiencing a peaceful night with a gentle breeze, but the city on the other side was many Americans' worst nightmare. Only worse. Terrorism by vampires? The ridiculous thought almost made Shrina laugh.

She made her way to the stairwell, past the barbeque that brought back memories of times visiting there with her parents. But that had been a lifetime ago, a version of herself she wondered if she'd still recognize if she met today. Prestige was right—the old "her" hadn't been a girl scout, not a role model in the slightest. But now? She was doing her best.

Getting into the SIG was certainly a step in the right direction.

She descended the stairs three at a time and emerged into a hallway that told a story of destruction and terror. It was clear someone had been there and had meant to do damage. Three bodies lined the hallway, the last just outside the door where Shrina was headed.

"Mrs. Aby," Shrina said, kneeling beside the neighbor. The woman had always been kind, and even covered in blood she had a peacefulness around her, staring up through her silver-framed glasses and matching hair.

"They were coming for your place," Mrs. Aby said as she tried to push herself up. "I wasn't having it."

Shrina reached out to help the woman, but Mrs. Aby fell back as the life drained from her eyes and they stared back hollow, distant… dead.

With a curse, Shrina was up and into her grandparents' home, arc rod ready, eyes searching for any sign of danger. What she found was an apartment torn to shreds. Chairs were on their sides, the walls had been gashed by what looked like claws, and the contents of the closets were scattered across the floor. What she didn't find was any sign of blood or corpses.

Prestige's tablet and school bag sat on her bed, untouched. Shrina grabbed the bag, threw the tablet inside, and went back to the hallway. The door opposite opened and a face she was beginning to worry she'd never see again stuck out around the doorframe. Her grandma!

"Oh, dear," her grandma said, stepping out cautiously and waving Shrina over.

Shrina ran over and hugged her, then said, "What happened?"

"They came for you," her grandma said. "I can't understand why, but for some reason, she wanted you."

"She?" Shrina asked.

Her grandma nodded, looking at her with curiosity. Shrina couldn't answer her questions though. Looking further into the room, she saw her grandpa and went to hug him, too, then told them both to come with her.

"I'll get you to safety," she said. "Prestige is on the roof. I have a pod."

Without argument, they quickly followed her out and up the stairs. Shrina explained that she had run into some of the attackers downstairs, but didn't have the slightest clue what was happening.

When they reached the pod, everyone hugged again before piling in. Shrina lifted off and headed toward Bethesda, hoping she'd be able to find Trent's dad's house again.

As they went, they talked about what they'd heard on the news since everything started. Some were saying it was vampires, demons from hell coming to punish them all for going after the forbidden fruit. Others speculated that these creatures had come through the gateway, or that somehow opening the gateway had caused mutations. Shrina's grandpa confirmed that the military was heavily involved—not just here but across the world. They had already started setting up safe havens for people who didn't feel their living situations were safe, and he recommended they find one of them.

"These safe havens won't likely be up for a bit," Shrina argued. "Let's try my idea first."

She got no arguments from them, which didn't surprise her. Ever since she'd moved back in with them, they'd seen her in a different light. She wasn't their little girl anymore but an intel agent. A woman of authority.

In moments like this, she appreciated it, but

sometimes wished she could just be that little girl again and be taken care of. She wanted to be told everything was going to be all right, but at the moment she knew that was her job.

When they finally made it to Bethesda, Trent's dad recognized her instantly, welcoming them in and quickly turning off the news. The chaos hadn't made it out there, he explained, and they should be safe. Shrina couldn't help but notice the rifle and the magazines he'd been in the process of loading.

"Just in case," he said when he noticed her look.

"Good," she replied.

"Hope you forgot to eat in all this chaos," he said, leading them to a dining room that sported a small chandelier and a table with a pristine white tablecloth. "The way I see it, the power could go off at any minute at times like these, so we need to eat the main perishables. I trust you can help me with that?"

Prestige smiled and nodded, and the fact that she was less talkative than normal wasn't missed. Trent's dad quickly started cooking, after setting out some cheese and a fine bottle of wine for the adults. He also found some sparkling cider for Prestige.

"We're going to be okay here," Shrina told her sister.

The girl—almost a young woman—stared up at her and said, "We'll do our best."

"I'll protect you."

"You have a job to do," Prestige said as she nodded to the living room and led the way. They left their grandparents sitting at the table, holding each other's hands as they bowed their heads and prayed. Once the girls were in the other room, she continued, "I know you'll have to go to work. Honestly, carrying on might be the best thing for us, and your job is too important to ignore."

"So you're the grown up here?" Shrina asked with a chuckle.

"You taught me well," Prestige replied.

"No, don't say that. Don't grow up too fast on account of me."

Prestige nodded, forced a smile, and turned to look at a picture of a younger Trent in a Marine Corps uniform. It looked like it had been taken at his boot camp graduation, and his dad stood next to him, full of pride.

"He'll be fine," she assured Shrina.

"We all will be," Shrina replied, as if the words were rehearsed. "Sorry, that came out wrong. I mean, we'll do our best, and so far in the history of humanity, that's seemed to work out okay."

"Inspiring words," Prestige said with a scoff. "But seriously, if I know boys, this one right here is a survivor."

"Oh, you know boys now?"

Prestige glanced back and shrugged.

"Shut up! Who?" Shrina sat back on the couch, wondering how the hell she'd missed this bit of knowledge. "Someone at school?"

Prestige leaned against the wall, hands in her pockets. If not for the silly grin on her face, she would've looked very grown up in that moment. "His name's Grant. Plays hockey."

"Is it serious?"

"Not as serious as his love of hockey, but getting there. Maybe. If I want it to."

"Yeah, okay." Shrina shifted uncomfortably. "Did… did they ever have the talk with you?"

"Oh my God, Shrina." Prestige stood up from the wall and tucked her hair behind her ears. "Yes, I'm old enough to know about all of that. Come on."

"Good, it's just… I know it's stupid with all of this going on, but be smart, okay?"

Prestige stared at her for a moment, then laughed. Shrina laughed, too, and was just about to open her mouth when her wrist piece showed an incoming call. It was her boss, Senior Agent Maison.

"Take it," Prestige said, her eyes showing understanding beyond her years. "I know it's important."

"Not as important as this," Shrina replied.

"Sis, if it's about saving the world, then shut up and take it."

Shrina moved to the foyer where she took the linked earpiece and attached it above her ear so she could hear without bothering the others.

"We need you here, bright and early," her boss explained, after checking on her safety.

"I don't understand," Shrina said. "People need to be with their families. You can't expect everyone to drop that and come running in."

"Not everyone," Maison said. "You, and a few select others."

"Wait, what? What for?"

The voice on the other end was silent for a moment, then said, "I'm not supposed to tell you that, Shrina."

"So…? I need to know it's worth it."

"You need to follow orders," he said, with a sigh. "But I get it. All I'll say is that they're going to ask you a question. They're looking for people who want to be part of this, a part of fighting whatever these things are."

She thanked him and said she'd be there first thing in the morning, then signed off and returned to her family.

"What is it?" Prestige asked.

"Work. They need me," Shrina answered.

"And we don't?" Grandma asked as she approached. Grandpa stood behind her, hand on the doorway.

"They need me to help get rid of this threat," Shrina explained, and the others knew there was no arguing with those words.

Prestige simply hugged her, and then their grandparents joined in.

"Be careful out there," her grandma said, kissing Shrina on the forehead as if she were a little girl again.

6

TRENT: SPACE, KRASTION GALAXY

Trent held tight to the control panel of his escape pod, hands pressed against it as if that would stop the rattling and jarring as it hurtled through space. He had no idea how long it'd been since his ship had broken apart because he'd passed in and out of consciousness several times. Still, he had hope. The pod's self-guidance and detection system had revealed a planet and was taking him toward it.

He had no way of knowing if this was the planet they'd set out for or one of several others in this star system. As he approached, he noted that it looked nothing like it should. There had been data to suggest other planets, but the agencies of Earth had yet to test them or even confirm their existence.

Could this one, like the other, be potentially inhabitable?

Quite unintentionally and a lot sooner than he had expected, he was about to find out the answer to that question.

Everyone was gone. He tried to push the thought aside once again, thinking instead about the attack on Earth and wondering what it had accomplished for the attackers. They'd taken two of the ships, but for what? Did they think they could come up here and colonize the planet before anyone else? The idea would've made Trent laugh if he didn't feel so sick.

They would've been attacked by whatever was behind those large, brightly glowing red eyes. The thought of those eyes haunted him now, each the size of three of their ships and surrounded by inescapable darkness. Even when he closed his own eyes, he saw them, staring. He recalled the rattling of the ship as it was hit and remembered the screams.

Had he been piloting the ship as he had wanted, he wouldn't have made it to the escape pod. How ironic that the one thing he'd really wanted in life was to pilot a ship, but the fact that he'd failed meant he was alive. Memories of cursing after finding out he hadn't been accepted to the pilot program, of sharing drinks over the moment with his friends, and of a mistaken relapse with Enise that night flashed through his mind, but he was too close to potential death to be able to laugh or even smile at the thought.

The escape pod spun again, giving him a view of the planet's gray and desolate surface. His heart sank.

Inside his Space-Fleet-Marine-issued suit, he'd have enough oxygen to survive for maybe two to three days, but they weren't built for much more than that. If a rescue mission didn't arrive before his time ran out, he was doomed. But judging by the speed with which he was approaching the planet's surface, none of that would likely matter. What good was oxygen if the fall killed him? And even if he did survive, how would a rescue mission reach him in time? The attack on his squadron had caught them all off guard.

The pod lurched and so did his stomach. Everything he had eaten that morning—if it could be called "morning" in space—came flying up and out, splattering the inside of the escape pod, and one long shout of panic shot forth before contact. He blacked out for a second, then was back as he felt himself tumbling over and over, jolt after jolt rocketing through the escape pod. His consciousness faded numerous times until, with wide eyes and almost perfect clarity, he saw a wall of ice before him. He tried to brace himself but found nothing to brace himself against. With the realization that this could be his last breath, he took a long one, tried to focus on all the pleasant moments in life, and then prepared to die.

The pod made impact, crashing through ice and rock, and throwing him into a dark cavern. Then it hit, and as he was flung forward he was out, darkness quickly taking over.

A groan. His eyes moved to his body armor as his mind processed what had just happened. His body ached with pain. He glanced around at the inside of the pod, wondering how long he'd been out.

What was he doing there? It was fuzzy but coming back. They were to get out there and find out if the planet could be Earth's first move toward colonization. Humans had extended their reach back on Earth, even on the space stations that were inhabited mostly by miners. Size wasn't so much an issue, but resources were. Space stations heavily relied on Earth, and terraforming on Mars and Titan had been going much slower than originally planned. That was why the Intergalactic Space Agency for Progress had designated teams for recon, many made up of flight captains to handle the crafts, scientists to make the determination, and Marines in case they met resistance.

Some laughed at the idea of having a Space Fleet Marine force at all. But ever since the global peace act had been formed on Earth and infighting between the planet and its space stations in what had been termed the "Biotech Wars" had ceased, all other forms of military had largely ceased along with it. Terrorism was inevitable but had become the jurisdiction of the small anti-terrorism cells of the new SIG, and was usually stopped before a concept could even evolve into an idea, let alone a plan.

Trent's family before him had all served in the military, dating all the way back to his great-grandfather in World War III, the war that had threatened to end all life on Earth. It was ironic that, having brought an end to wars and large-scale violence, World War III had also created the overpopulation problem that now forced them to search for other inhabitable planets.

All of this went through Trent's mind as he groaned, trying to undo his harness. Realizing that wasn't going to happen, he reached behind him, found his Ka-Bar knife, and sawed through the thick restraint. When he was free, his first action was to slam the button at the side of the chair. A whirring sounded, followed moments later by sections of the chair moving aside so that his Space Marine armor could snap into place. Within minutes, he was fully geared up and ready to go. He just needed the helmet.

Pressing a button at the top of the pod, he leaned back and watched as the helmet casing lowered. He reached into it, pulled out the golden helmet with its red globe and anchor embossed on the side—a wink to the fact that the U.S. had been the first to get this global force up and running—and secured the helmet into place.

He checked to ensure everything was safe and then said, "Computer, I'll need air here. Going out."

There was no response but a simple beeping, and then his helmet clicked and his HUD screen read, in blinking green letters: *Proceed Gunnery Sergeant Helms.*

Protection from whatever was out there would be great, but for now he could only focus on escaping the stench of his vomit, still dripping from the control panel. It hurt to move, but the armor acted as an exoskeleton that helped by supporting his legs when they wanted to give out. He made his way to the hatch and pulled the lever down at its side, revealing the code for the exit. After hurtling about like he had, he now understood why they kept that exit button so protected. The last thing anyone wanted was to escape, only to be hurled out into space because they'd accidentally pressed a button with their elbow.

He stepped into the doorway and was about to step out when he paused, arms thrust out to stop himself from falling. The whole escape pod was at an angle over a giant precipice. A gust of wind rattled the pod and he cursed, glancing about for a way out of his predicament. If he could climb onto the top of the pod and maybe make it back out that way, he could—

"AHHH!" he screamed as another gust of wind caused the pod to rattle, harder this time, interrupting his thoughts. He reached out for the hold above the door, only to see the pod break free from the surrounding rock and ice, and fall.

He was falling with it, half out the door, and managed to turn to see the ground approaching far away.

Mind spinning a million light-years a second, he pushed on the top of the doorway and kicked out with one boot, initiating the thrusters that were an integral part of the boot's design. Suddenly, he was back in the pod screaming, "Door, close!"

There was nowhere else to be in there except for the seat, but when he reached to fasten himself in, he remembered that he had cut the harness. Before he had time for another thought, the pod impacted with a thud that threw him into the dashboard, smashing it to bits.

Luckily, he was wearing the armor, and even though it hurt like hell, he was fairly certain nothing was broken. A pain crept into his stomach, and he realized that the impact had jostled around the goods downstairs a tad too much. If he ever made it back, he'd have to remember to tell base command to add extra padding down there.

With a groan, he pushed himself back up, opened the door again, and managed to squeeze between the doorway and the ground. It was an earthy ground, he was surprised to see, and gave to his touch. He looked around in the darkness and worried for a moment. What if whatever had attacked them back on Earth was also here on this planet? Something had certainly attacked them when they'd crossed over through the gateway, and he had to assume it was all related.

He continued on, initiating the light in his left forearm. Even though it was still dark in the large cavern, at least now he could make out the walls, slick in their reflection of the light. His eyes were still adjusting, but he came out into a large open area and could've sworn he saw something move. With so much of the place covered in darkness, that didn't bode well for him. Now he wasn't only in pain and confused from the fall, but his chest was thumping and his temples sweating at the idea of something down there with him.

A roaring sounded ahead, and for a moment he worried that he'd stumbled upon the attackers' hide-out. Maybe it was a ship or something powering up, ready to attack his rescue party. That seemed logical, except now he was drawing closer and he was certain he recognized that sound. But from where?

As the darkness of the cavern walls curved, he saw what he assumed to be a massive opening leading out of the cave just ahead. Finally, there was a way for him to exit the place. The darkness led out into an area where light shone down from above. He approached the light and the roar with caution, and then, just as he saw the lush greenery, he suddenly realized why he knew that sound—it was a waterfall!

Each step he took was a bounding leap as he ran, stopping in the light where he could see water cascading down the side of a great cliff. As he looked around, he saw that all manner of trees and grasses covered the surrounding hills. His initial landing site must have been a completely different location altogether—just the side of a mountain range, he guessed. And if there were trees and running water, that meant there had to be oxygen, right?

After a moment of standing there enjoying the

sight, he remembered that his suit had an atmospheric tester built in. He opened up the display on his HUD, told it to run the test, and waited.

Atmospheric Match: Positive.

Well, hot damn! That was potentially good news, but he still wasn't sure he could trust it. With the beating his suit had taken, he half-wondered if it could be malfunctioning. Taking a deep, worried breath, he pressed the button on his helmet that pulled back the faceplate, leaving his face exposed.

He didn't evaporate or burn up or whatever else he supposed might happen if the atmosphere hadn't been hospitable. Instead, he took a huge breath of clean, pure air. It was unlike any air he had ever breathed before, as if someone had taken air and opened it up, filling it with more air. It had a slight chill to it and cooled him from the inside out.

Wind blew through the trees, causing the leaves to rustle. Trent spun, watching the wind carry the foliage in a gentle way that made him think of spirits dancing across the treetops. He wasn't sure how long a rescue would take or whether such a mission would even happen, but for now, at least, his chances of survival had increased a great deal.

7

ESPINOZA: UNKNOWN PLANET A

After a night of attempting to sleep, the team built up fortifications and got to work on alterations to the comms systems. Espinoza enjoyed watching Kim work—a slight distraction from their predicament. Kim said she could do something using scrap from other areas of the ship that hadn't been damaged by the explosion and possibly get them to send a signal. The engine was fried, but not all the electronics were, at least.

Espinoza wasn't a tech genius, though he was a "comms guy" and knew how to operate the systems when the time came. He was actually a cryptologic analyst, meaning he was trained in sending and receiving specially classified messages, and he'd been included on this mission in case they found information that was deemed highly confidential. He held a higher clearance than Ellins. Though the captain would have the same access, he was a pilot and wouldn't know much about Espinoza's world.

"Who's up?" Captain Thomas said, finally able to get on his feet. Normally more talkative and full of vigor, this whole experience seemed to have hit him harder than the rest, maybe because he didn't have his buddy, Aarol, there with him.

"I'm not having any luck here," Kim said, stepping out from the ship and wiping her brow with the back of her hand. "Could use a breather, chance to stretch my legs."

"Right. You and Espinoza then."

She nodded and jogged over to grab her rifle, then joined Espinoza at the edge of the water pile, which was a stack of canteens against the edge of the ship's water supply, half of which had survived the explosion.

"We spotted anything there yet?" she asked.

"If we had, you don't think you would've heard about it?" Espinoza replied.

"I'm not in the loop much since I'm always tinkering over there."

"Yeah, well, nothing yet."

The two started out, picking a direction the last three teams hadn't gone and slinging their rifles over their shoulders. The weapons hit the magnetic holders with a clunk, ready to be pulled free when necessary.

After the first dune of orange and red dirt, they went past some low hills and found a field of more densely growing grass, along with some of those weird tulip trees. They worked in a spiral motion, checking the surrounding area without straying too far from base. More hills rose up in the distance, and Espinoza found himself wondering what might be in the caves in those hills, if there were any. His imagination threw ideas at him like in the old films with large animals living just beneath the surface.

More than once, he noticed Kim's eyes glancing over at him, as if she didn't think he could see through her faceplate.

"What?" he finally asked when he saw her looking for the fourth or fifth time.

"You think we're getting off this rock?" she asked.

"Um, you're the one fixing the comms."

"Trying," she corrected him. "I'm... not hopeful."

"Well, shit."

She nodded.

They walked on a bit and he sighed. "The others are right—Franco, I mean. Earth will send a rescue mission. They'll have to. We just have to survive until then."

"Yeah, of course."

For a while they walked in silence, still finding no sign of anyone or anything living, aside from the local flora. They watched as the sky blurred with a mist that settled in just above them. Heavy winds picked up, whistling through the hills.

"Your last meal before coming out here," Kim said, glancing around and then back to him with a grin. "What was it?"

"What?"

"Humor me. Talking about normal shit calms my nerves. And right now, I need a lot of damn calming."

He chuckled and thought back to it. "Before heading out, my parents met me at this fancy steak joint. Had myself the best rib eye I've ever had in my life."

"Medium rare?"

"Hell no. Rare, baby."

She grinned. "My kinda man." Her smile faded. "I didn't mean it like, well, you know."

He laughed at her awkwardness, then asked, "You?"

"Three slices of banana cream pie."

"For dinner?"

She grinned, getting back into the comfort of the discussion. "I was too nervous, and my family couldn't make it out because of a storm, and well… my dad's sick. So I said whatever, it's my night, and went out to treat myself. When the lady at the diner started going on about specials and whatnot, all I could do was stare at the dessert menu with that damn picture of banana cream pie. When I'd had the first, it was so good I had to have a second."

"And the third?" Espinoza asked.

She shrugged. "At that point, I realized I might not have it again for a very long time. I figured I'd better have another slice to try and make myself sick so I wouldn't want it anytime soon."

"And that worked?"

"Hell no. I'd kill for a slice right now," she admitted and licked her lips.

He glanced over, looking her up and down, then laughed when caught. "Sorry, it's just that…"

"You were checking to see if I'm fat?" She waved him off. "Please, my genes don't allow it. Plus, now that we're enhanced, haven't you noticed that we can eat whatever we want and burn it off much faster?"

"I hadn't thought about it."

"Right now, tell me," she said and leaned in, as if it were a secret. "One kind of cake or pie. What would it be?"

"Tres leches. Not even a question."

"Trez what?"

He blinked, turning to her with surprise. "Tres leches. Three milks, I guess. It's… oh my God, it's the best cake in the world. You've never had it?"

She frowned, shaking her head.

"I'm buying you a slice when we get back," he said and glanced around the planet, looking at the sparse grass in the distance and the swaying, strange-looking trees, "or maybe we'll find some version of milk and flour and all that here, and we can find a way to make one."

"When we have to colonize the place ourselves because we're stranded here, you mean?"

"No, I'm not…" He froze for two reasons—the first had been the thought of what she'd just said and the implication that the males and females would procreate at some point. But while that image went through his mind, his eyes focused on something else.

"Everything okay?" she asked.

"You see something over—" Espinoza started to ask, then yelped and pulled Kim to the ground.

A four-round burst tore into the tree behind them, and then they were rolling, preparing to return fire. They saw flashes of movement. Something was up and visible, then immediately down again. Espinoza stared over the sights of his DD4 rifle, freaking out that not only had the shots been the same four-round burst his DD4 made, but he'd caught a glimpse just then and was pretty sure that what he'd seen was human.

"Others made it," he said, his voice low and uncertain.

"What?" Kim asked, moving her rifle from side to side, about to have a panic attack.

"The other ships. Those are ours out there, shooting at us." Espinoza took a chance and knelt with his rifle in the air, then shouted, "We're on the same side. It's Sergeant Espinoza and—"

There was an answering burst of shots and one even hit his rifle, knocking it back into the orange dirt. He fell back and then scrambled over to it, recovering it in time to see Kim shooting.

"Stop! Stop!" he shouted but then saw a round hit someone. The person wasn't wearing the Marine armor but a gray and blue uniform with exoskeleton and chest plate. It wasn't one of theirs after all but whoever had attacked them at the launch.

Espinoza readied his rifle, too, lying prone and firing. Two more shots connected and then the figure was turning back, another appearing to help him. Kim and Espinoza popped up, running forward in pursuit as they fired, but there was no sign of either of their opponents.

"Tell me I didn't just imagine all that," Kim said, ducking down in case more attackers were nearby.

Espinoza followed suit but kept his rifle up, scanning the horizon, looking for any sight of them. "We're seeing ghosts now?"

"Or... they're just that fast," she countered.

"Nobody's *that* fast. Not even us."

"Well, *your* explanation is ghosts, so..."

He chuckled, not really in the mood for laughing but seeing the humor there. "True, true. You win; they're fast. But how do we explain it to the rest?"

"We let Gunny decide," she said.

Espinoza agreed, so they pulled back. On the way, he marked their position on a nearby tree. They weren't halfway back when the storm picked up. It wasn't just winds at that point. It was debris, heavy clouds, and a distant rumbling. Strong winds came first, picking up the dirt and whipping it against their armor and faceplates.

At least they didn't have to worry about the other attackers in the storm, he figured.

8

SHRINA: SHARED INTELLIGENCE GROUP, AMERICAN BRANCH

As much as Shrina wanted to be with her family right then, she knew the need to watch over them was purely emotional at this point. The National Guard had come in and set up barriers. Secret Service was being assisted by the Marines to secure important personnel, and Trent's father had agreed to take her family in until this all blew over or go to one of the safety zones if necessary.

"Take care of them," she'd told Prestige when giving her a hug early the next morning, leaving before the rest were up.

Nobody asked questions when she arrived in a police pod, and the guard simply nodded at her explanation. Her stealing a police pod certainly hadn't been the craziest thing that had happened the night before.

So far, there'd been no sign of Senior Agent Maison, so she wasn't sure he was going to make it. She'd been escorted to a large conference room that had been gutted, leaving only herself and the other dozen or so men and women to stand around and wait.

"What is this?" one of the women said. She was tall and had a shaved head. "Which of you knows?"

Nobody spoke up.

She grunted and glanced around for a window, then turned back to glare at each of them when she saw there were no windows. Shrina glared back and the woman raised an eyebrow. After a moment, she nodded, then continued to scan the room. There was something about this woman Shrina liked, so she made a note to stay close to her when everything got crazy.

A door banged open from the side of the room, causing half of those gathered to jump. Who could blame them after the night they'd had?

"All right," a tall man with slicked-back hair said as he entered. He had the type of stubble that clearly wasn't a fashion statement but a result of working too long without a break. Judging by the look in his eyes, he'd gotten about as much sleep as the rest of them, which wasn't much. "Here's what we know. There shouldn't be a need for me to say this, but nothing we say from here on leaves this room."

"Let me guess," a woman said who looked to be a couple of years younger than Shrina and a good foot shorter, "you're going to tell us those things were actual vampires?"

He glared at her and then continued, not even acknowledging the joke, if that's what it was. "Even though we were able to take a few of them down, it appears that others came in and took their bodies before we had a chance to bring them in for study."

"Or they came back from the dead," the woman said. "You know… vampires."

"What's your name?" the man demanded of her.

"Cindy," she said with a grin, then glanced around, seeming to suddenly remember where she was. "Special Agent Chung."

"Right, Agent Chung. I'm Agent Richards. Now that we're friends, feel free to make all the jokes you want when we've killed the enemy, but right now I want to assure you that they aren't vampires, no matter what the media is saying. Our best bet—"

"Genetic modifications," Shrina offered, cutting him off.

He looked at her, but she couldn't tell if it was

respect or contempt in his eyes. "Yes, that's correct. Shrina Collins, isn't it?"

"Yes, sir."

"Well, you're correct. It's no secret among us that New Origins first perfected the super-soldier formula, or that the U.S. Government has been adapting it, experimenting. It's not unheard of that someone else has gotten their hands on some left-over New Origins tech. I don't know the details, but that's what we're all assuming for now."

"And the glowing eyes? Teeth?" a young man asked.

Richards shook his head and a flash of uncertainty showed before he regained his composure. "Terrorist tactics designed to scare us. Plankton or fish or whatever glow in certain parts of the world. It's called bioluminescence. I don't know. Maybe the teeth... maybe they were crossed with some sort of animal DNA, or they simply had a fancy tooth job done at the local dentist."

Shrina frowned while others offered nervous laughter. She could see it being a result of alterations to genetic modifications, but the explanation felt like it was missing part of the puzzle.

"What we're talking about here," Richards said, turning to look at each of them, "isn't about trying to hypothesize what these things are. We're here to get a joint strike team out there—Marines, SIG, and more—to hunt these bastards down and make them pay for this attack."

"Oorah," one of the men said.

"That's right. And you know the Marines' saying, Semper Fi? Semper Fidelis, always faithful. Well, we're going to ask that of you here and now—those of you who sign up. We're not only talking about super secretive operations; we're talking about giving you the same mods those Marines had who went into space, maybe better. Some of it is still, shall we say, experimental. You'd be stronger, faster, quicker to heal."

He kept talking about the ways training would happen, but Shrina's mind focused on her sister and Marick, about their modifications and how she'd seen them move, along with their friend Pete. She'd had dreams of being able to leap that high, punch with the power of several men, and heal much faster than should be humanly possible.

Even if the idea of revenge against these genetic mutations wasn't on the table, she would've volunteered just to get the mods. Since both were her rewards here, she stood when he asked for volunteers, eager to be among the first responders.

"I accept, sir," Shrina said when he came to her in order, confirming her decision.

"From what I hear about you," he said, clasping her hand in his, "it'll be an honor to have you on the team."

She grinned, then followed the others out. It hit her that this meant leaving her sister behind and she hated that. Still, this had to be done. Prestige was in good hands and wasn't exactly a child anymore.

The world needed her, and her sister was included in that equation. Even though the emotional part of her knew being apart would suck, she was doing this for Prestige as much as anyone. Shrina couldn't let those monsters live in the same world as her sister.

They didn't waste any time, either. After signing the necessary paperwork, Shrina was brought to another facility, along with a couple of dozen others. The room was part of a clean, state-of-the-art tech and medical facility, and the back room had pods lined up in a way that made it all feel very much like it was part of some fancy resort.

Nobody glanced around awkwardly or acted like a horny teenager when they were told to strip. They were all eager to do their part for humanity, and although she was very much aware of the nudity around her, she didn't look. That wasn't what they were there for. She also wasn't embarrassed or ashamed because all of this was bigger than the flesh.

They were told to enter their pods, where they settled in and had cables attached to them via straps. The pod doors closed and she felt a pinch in her arm and a sharp pain in her thigh before darkness descended as she was put under for the remainder of the treatment.

While she was under, Shrina saw flashes of dreams but nothing complete—a river, gusts of wind, and trees blowing over. The images kept coming but then faded as a storm took over, and it became gray and dark. Out of that storm, a voice spoke. "At last... at long last... you have returned." She knew it was only a dream but felt hatred for that voice, a revulsion she couldn't explain. Distantly, she was aware of her body struggling, wanting to be free, to escape the pod and the upgrades, but she couldn't. She was flying forward through those stormy clouds, and there was something moving through them but hidden. It clung to her in a non-physical way, pulling her along, and then the clouds vanished and she was in an ancient cave. The walls were covered with etchings, murals, and old paintings, some inlaid with gold and decorated with rubies and other precious gems.

All of these artifacts led her to the rear of the cave where a final piece of art displayed a dragon rising up on its hind legs, and it had rubies for eyes.

The eyes started to come alive, staring at her and calling for her. She tried to turn, to run, to thrash about and escape.

And then, with a gasp, she was awake and someone was pulling her from the pod, her nude body limp in their arms. She was aware of having returned and that she was in the room with the upgrade pods, but she couldn't move her body. Someone had wrapped something around her, or maybe draped something over her, and she was on the floor. A couple of the others were leaning over her, asking if she was okay, but all she could do was moan and stare out at what she knew was the ceiling but seemed to her to be the dragon's eyes staring back at her.

"This has never happened," a voice said, distantly.

"Dammit, find out what's going on!" Richards said, and then he paused, noticing that she had shifted.

Being able to hear them more clearly now helped bring her back to the moment. She blinked as the image of the dragon faded, and she moved her head from side to side. A couple of the other agents hadn't even bothered to get dressed yet—a fact that didn't provide the best view from her angle.

"Agent Collins," Richard said, taking her hand. "Are you with us? Can you hear me?"

"I'm—I'm fine," she said, still trying to process. "What happened?"

"We don't know," one of the technicians said. "As I was explaining, a—"

"It's never happened before," she cut him off, starting to sit up. "Yeah, I got that."

"Er…" Richards said and turned his head to look away.

Shrina glanced down to see why. She'd forgotten she was still nude but for his jacket draped over her. She quickly covered back up, blushing. It hadn't bothered her before that they'd had to get nude for the upgrades, but now, being the center of attention was a different story.

"Right, everyone," Richards said. "Suit up. Nothing to see here."

"Hey," she protested, before even realizing she'd said it.

"I didn't mean…" He glanced her way, frowned, and then laughed. "Really?"

She shrugged and stood, feeling a bit wobbly, but she'd be okay. Even as she walked over to her uniform, her strength was coming back. It had just been a dream—a very real, very impactful dream. At least, she had to believe that. Of course, that's all it was.

Every movement now was tainted by her confusion, and she felt self-conscious from all that attention coming her way. She quickly pulled on her panties and then her bra, glancing back to see that she was just being paranoid. Nobody was watching her.

With a deep sigh, she slipped on her uniform and boots, and then joined the others where they were forming up in the next room over. She was the last to arrive, but nobody made anything of it. How could they, considering what she'd just gone through? They all likely thought she had a medical condition. Every one of them was probably wondering if she really belonged there, and she resented them for it.

"Welcome, ladies and gentlemen," Richards said, looking at each of them in turn, "to Project Rebirth. Maybe you're all wondering what you've just gotten yourselves into, but trust me when I say that what's out there needs to be dealt with. We don't know what it is, but you are going to find out. We're talking the best equipment and information available. And yes, you'll be putting yourself in harm's way. However…"

At this he stopped, smiled, and pulled a Ka-Bar from his side, then jammed it into his own forearm! Most of the group cringed, one woman yelped, and Shrina laughed. She'd seen others healing from injuries. She hadn't realized it yet, but of course Richards would already have the upgrades.

He nodded her way, then pulled the knife out. He clearly still felt pain—his eyes were tearing up and he shook for a second—and then the flesh started healing. Everyone stared, mumbling to each other in their confusion, and some stepped forward to get a better look when the skin healed over. The whole process couldn't have taken more than thirty seconds.

"No way," one of the men said and took a step back, his mind clearly trying to process what he'd just witnessed.

"Way, Agent Drakes," Richards said, then showed them that the knife still had his blood on it. "Not a trick, not makeup. This is what your body is capable of now. Still, we imagine you'll want to avoid getting injured as much as possible since there are limits. You can't regenerate a limb, for example, and you certainly won't re-grow your head."

A couple of nervous chuckles followed.

"Plus armor and shields," he added.

"Fine. That's all great," Shrina said, speaking up, "but where do we start? Do we have anything to go off of?"

Richards frowned and was about to answer when Drakes started coughing. At first it was just an annoying interruption, but the third time Richards tried to speak, Drakes fell over, retching and coughing. Blood spattered the floor as Richards called for the techs and a doctor, but by the time the techs had come charging in, Drakes was on the floor, his last breath leaving him.

"Dead," one of them confirmed.

"What the hell?" Richards pushed the guy out of the way to check for a pulse himself, not caring about stepping in the blood. Shrina was in a state of almost full-blown shock, but she'd seen death before so this was more surprise and confusion like everyone else there was feeling.

"Nobody noticed this?" the other tech said, pointing to a scabbed-over wound on Drake's exposed arm.

"Is it important?" the other asked, stepping in to see.

"Bite marks," the first replied, then looked up at Richards. "Sharp teeth. I'd be willing to bet our boy here was bitten by one of those things. Those—for want of a better term—vampires."

"This isn't a game," Richards said, shaking his head. "You're telling me a bite from one of those things killed him? Get someone out there to see if others have been bitten and if the same thing's happening to them."

"And if not?" the tech said, glancing from Richards to each of the rest, frown deepening.

Shrina had realized the implication immediately, and swearing from around the room confirmed that the others had started to figure it out. It had happened shortly after receiving the upgrades. It was a big assumption, but it was possible that upgrading them had made them susceptible to whatever the hell it was that those vampires carried in their blood.

She stared at the body, suddenly feeling much less excited about going on the hunt.

9

TRENT: UNKNOWN PLANET B

Trent had been walking, exploring his new home. It was like a dream version of Earth, like something he'd seen on a poster or with simulation goggles when playing games with his friends. But here he was, really living it.

Each step was a reminder that he'd survived but also that he was lost. Alone. He started regretting everything he'd failed at in life—notably relationships. His mother had passed a few years back, and his father could have used more company. He'd barely seen the man since the time he'd brought his ex-girlfriend over to meet him, something he'd have to remedy if he ever made it back.

That day at his dad's had left him with pleasant memories, at least. His dad had taken him aside after dinner and said, "That one there, she's a catch. Not looks, or not *only* looks, I mean. Take care of her, son, because I see the way she looks at you… and you don't want to lose that."

Knowing that the man was still grieving Trent's mom made those words even harder to ignore later when he and Shrina had finally broken up. He would've loved to stay with her, but life got in the way. That seemed like a stupid excuse now, although he had to remind himself that if they'd still been together, she'd be worried sick about him right then. It was part of the reason they'd broken up in the first place. But he'd dated others since then, such as Enise, so why was he thinking about Shrina? That ship had sailed long ago. Maybe it was because Enise had been on this mission and he didn't want to have to consider what might have happened to her. Or maybe, although he hated this thought, maybe Enise had never held that same spot in his heart.

A glance around showed the trees shifting in the breeze. He held out his arms, feeling the coolness against his face as he smiled and took it all in.

Any thoughts of enjoying the moment fled as a confused combination of fright and hope took over because the moving trees had revealed something he almost couldn't believe. Past one of the hills and up on a ridge, he'd spotted a reflection of light. Looking closer as the trees moved aside again, there was no doubt in his mind—there was a ship up there, likely one from his team. If someone was alive, anyone beside himself, he was going to piss his pants with joy.

10

ESPINOZA: SPACE, UNKNOWN PLANET A

Orange dirt and debris flew about, winds whipping and howling, but Espinoza and Kim had their Marine armor to protect them. His HUD was alive with warnings, but all he wanted it to do was confirm that they were on the right track back to their base. His legs were aching from nonstop running, and his mind was thudding with the stress of one thought—he had no idea where they were.

Their situation wasn't made any better by Kim shouting, "You're going the wrong way!" through the comms.

"Take the lead whenever you'd like," he replied.

She angrily gestured for him to keep going, clearly as lost as he was. It didn't bother him, though. He figured he'd see a landmark or maybe find someone from the team sooner or later, or maybe the comms would connect. The storm was causing a lot of interference, but more than once he'd been certain he'd heard a voice.

What worried him was that some of the hills seemed to have shifted. He focused on his surroundings, looking for patterns. In land nav classes and when traversing actual terrain during his military training back home, he'd never had a problem and had always been at the top of his class, so for him to be lost like this felt out of place.

The wind picked up and the dirt in the air was like a heavy fog, the hills showing and vanishing in bursts of brief visibility.

With her next step, Kim went sprawling forward and then started to fall backward. Espinoza lunged for her, catching her by the hand and pulling her up to see that they were at the edge of a drop-off, dirt falling and then catching in the wind. It was hard to see how far it went, but these two didn't care to stay and find out. They kept on running, trying to contact the team. No luck.

Something moved, but Espinoza couldn't be certain it wasn't just the dirt and the shadows. Again there was movement—something large and terrifying. He couldn't explain it, but he knew he wanted nothing to do with the thing.

"There!" Espinoza said as the dirt in the air let up somewhat. He pointed to the base of one of the nearby hills where he was fairly certain he'd just seen a cave. "Shelter!"

They pushed through the storm, winds so strong that even in their armor and with their enhanced strength they were having trouble moving. Something was coming at them and Espinoza had lifted his rifle to fire when whatever it was swept up and nearly hit him in the head. All they saw was a silhouette in the dirt or maybe a piece of wood. They couldn't be sure.

Kim pulled him along, arm up to protect her head even with the helmet. That was a smart move, he realized. No reason to take chances.

"We're not going to make it," she said through the comms. "Not at this rate!"

"Thrusters?" he suggested.

"You leave the ground, you're not coming back," she said.

She'd made what was possibly a good point, but her mentioning the ground had given him an idea. "Get close to the ground," he said, "and lean forward, like we're climbing a hill. We'll be moving into the wind but at a forty-five-degree angle instead of straight on."

"Like when fighting a riptide!" she said, getting it.

They course-corrected and got low to the ground, providing less of a friction point for the wind, and soon were making for the hills at twice the speed. A tree branch flew by and then another came right for Kim. Espinoza threw himself at her, thrusters on, hoping to hell she hadn't been right about flying off. He knocked her aside and the branch hit his boot, throwing him feet-first into the air.

He couldn't believe it but the wind was keeping him up like that, even with all his armor. Kim reached and snagged hold of him by the chest piece, then pulled him back to the ground with her.

"Together," she shouted and they went like that, clinging to each other.

The wind was still howling at the side of the hill but wasn't quite as strong, and in no time at all they reached the cave. It was narrow but deep—perfect for evading a storm. As they went in, rifles at the ready, they checked all directions but saw no signs of life. Their HUDs didn't pick up anything either.

The cave curved back like an "L," with a ridge toward the back. Someone or something very likely could have lived there once, but since they weren't there anymore, it would do.

Stowing their rifles, they turned to each other, laughing.

"I can't believe we survived that," he said.

"Well, so far," Kim replied. "But yeah, let's celebrate the little things in life."

After another glance toward the mouth of the cave, she took off her helmet and pulled her hair out, shaking it loose. Then she started pulling off her armor.

"What're you doing?" he said with a hiss.

"We're out of the storm, and by my guess, we'll be stuck here for a while." She wiped her brow, and he realized she'd been sweating, probably just as worried as he'd been. "When it's over, we'll get back out there, find the others, and see what to do about this other force."

"It's not right," he said, shaking his head. "Who'd they take out to get here?"

"Maybe they were here to begin with," she said.

He didn't know how to respond to that, instead simply watching her. He couldn't help but notice the way her uniform clung to her, accentuating her curves as she knelt to set her armor aside.

When she turned back to him, she smiled and said, "Strip."

"Huh?" he said, nearly choking.

"The armor, I mean," she added with a grin. "Nobody's coming in here through that. Might as well be comfortable."

Espinoza hesitated but then joined her by taking off his armor. He imagined he stunk like hell, what with all the running around, and he wished their suits had built-in showers. When he was done, he joined her where she sat on a rock ledge, looking out at the bend in the cavern where they could see bits of dirt still flying in from the storm.

She leaned in, head on his shoulder, and wrapped her arms around him.

"What… are you doing?" he asked.

"Seeking comfort in the arms of a big, strong man. Now shut up and put your arm around me."

He did, and they sat there for a while, watching the dirt accumulate. The wind continued to howl, and the sound of blowing dirt and debris caused a constant grinding sound.

"You ever hit the slopes?" she asked.

"No."

"It's like this, sometimes. Well, not the crazy alien planet or fear of death, but the way you can't see so well. I was in a blizzard once on Crystal Mountain in the Northwest, and it was like that. Must've been twelve or so, and I was there with my girl, Donica. I remember this one time, we were trying to find our way down in it and suddenly she vanishes. All I can think is 'shit, she's dead,' and I wanted to get out of there, to ride to the bottom and scream for help. But I knew she might need me, and that maybe, if I went down there... she wouldn't make it..."

She'd lost herself in the moment, so after a beat Espinoza said, "Did she?"

Kim licked her lips, glanced over, and took a breath. "Thing is, if I had gone flying down that hill like I wanted, I would've hit the same ledge she did. She'd conked her head and was dizzy, but I unstrapped and made my way down to her. I don't know... it's like if I hadn't, she might have just drifted off to sleep and been buried by the snow. In a way, I saved her because I didn't flee."

"Shit."

"Shit's right," she said with a laugh. "It's a big part of why I joined the Marines and a big part of why I wanted to be in space."

"To save lives?"

"To be there in case anyone needs their life saved, sure," she said. "But also because it was Donica's dream. Even though she lived, she also fractured her ankle in that fall. They told her she couldn't join."

Espinoza glanced over. "That's deep."

She shrugged. "Your turn."

"Why I joined?" he said and glanced away, then stared out at the dirt again. "Nothing as touching as all that. I thought it would help me get girls."

"Shut up," she said, hitting him lightly on the shoulder.

"I'm dead serious!" he said, rubbing the spot where she'd hit him. "I was chubby before I joined, never even had a girlfriend. Mock me all you want, but—as stupid as it sounds—that was my thought at the time. I could join, get in shape, and get to see space. And girls would dig it."

She laughed, stopped to look at him, and then laughed again. "Hey, at least it worked."

He cocked his head. "Did it?"

She bit her lower lip, staring at him. Another moment of silence followed, and then she sniffed.

"Just FYI," she said, breaking the relative silence. "You smell like hell."

"I was wondering if you'd noticed," he said with a chuckle.

"What, no comment about me stinking?" She leaned over and smelled her own armpit. "Gah."

"I happen to be a gentleman," he replied but honestly hadn't noticed.

She nuzzled him again, head on his shoulder, but then he glanced down and saw she was staring up at him.

"What?" he asked. "Trying to figure out how to tell me you're sorry for saying I stink?"

She pushed her head up and kissed him. It was a

gentle kiss—just her lips lightly brushing against his—but enough to make him imagine so much more.

"What was that about?" he asked when she had returned to resting her head on his shoulder.

"Just a test."

"A test?" he said with a frown. "Did I pass or fail?"

"A bit of both."

He scrunched his nose, trying to figure out what that meant, but then felt her hand moving up along his leg until it brushed along his crotch. A tingle went up his spine, and she was looking at him again.

"This is another test?" he asked.

She nodded, squeezing gently. "Let's see if you pass this time."

He wasn't sure what she meant but took the gamble. Turning to her, he placed a hand on her back and helped lower her to the ground. He straddled her and leaned in to start kissing her neck while she continued to caress him, and then he was caressing her, too, and they were ripping each other's stinky uniforms off.

All while the storm raged on outside.

11

SHRINA: SHARED INTELLIGENCE GROUP, AMERICAN BRANCH

Shrina thought that getting used to her enhancements should've taken longer than it had, but there she was, moving through the obstacle room Richards had set up to display his team. The government wasn't sending anyone without knowing what they were sending and that they were genuine badasses.

So far, the incident with Drakes had been brushed under the rug, dismissed as a one-off. The vampires had certainly killed others and had even left some alive who'd been bitten. None of those who'd survived that had shown signs of anything out of the ordinary—yet. Then again, none of *them* had been given the upgrades. It seemed suspicious, and the annoyance at it not being further investigated pushed Shrina harder, so that when she finished and leaped off of the last obstacle to land and face off against her sparring partner, she hit him too hard and sent him flying into the wall, ten feet back.

"I think we've seen enough," a voice said over the comms, slightly recognizable as Richards.

She nodded and turned to walk off but then stopped herself. This wasn't like her. Going back to her partner, she put out a hand to help him up.

"Sorry about that."

"I'll heal," he said, standing up and brushing himself off, "though I'm less certain of my pride."

She gave him a smile and was about to turn around again when he said, "Wait. Collins, right?"

"Shrina works," she replied, blurting it out but not sure why.

"Sure. Shrina, then. I'm Roy. Or Agent Peterson, whichever you prefer." He gestured for her to go ahead. "Hit up the showers. I'll wait so you have time to finish."

"Don't treat me like that," she replied. "I kicked your ass."

He laughed. "You're not afraid I'll sneak a peek?"

"We're professionals," she replied. "They wouldn't have done the showers that way otherwise."

"Or they're cheap," he said but shrugged and went along with her. "Something tells me you knew how to fight even before you were enhanced."

"I knew a bit before, but about a year ago I was in a crazy situation, and it reminded me that I needed to get serious about knowing how to defend myself. So I did."

"Oh, damn... Wait, you're that agent who was involved in the takedown of New Origins. I've heard about you."

With a shrug she pushed open the locker room doors, heading in and moving an aisle over. Like a gentleman, he went to the opposite aisle.

"That was you though, right?" he called out.

"I was involved, yeah," she replied as she pulled off her training shirt and bra. "It was mostly my sister and her husband, though."

"And they don't know where they all are?" he said as he walked past with a towel around his waist. He'd forgotten that she was changing and quickly looked away. "I mean, it's really true that all the old super soldiers up and left? Just kind of vanished?"

She frowned, not liking that he'd just seen her tits but knowing she'd been the one to insist on him not waiting. As she finished undressing and wrapping a towel around herself, she said, "That's the rumor, yeah. I think they all just wanted to go back to their normal lives."

When she finished, she walked past him to the showers while he found one on the other side. She glanced up, about to say something, and saw him hanging the towel, fully exposed. Damn. Well, at least they were even, she supposed.

He turned then, saw her looking, and frowned. Stepping out of her line of sight and into the shower, he started to wash. An awkward silence followed.

"I didn't mean to," she said, horrified.

"Don't mention it," he replied.

"No, I feel like a big perv." She hung her towel and got into the shower, starting to wash herself. She was glad he couldn't see her blushing in there. "I swear, that wasn't my intent."

"Hey, you saw something you liked and you couldn't look away. I get it."

"Shut up," she said with a laugh. "I swear, it was an accident."

The showers ran for a few more minutes with no further conversation, and then he stepped out. She stayed there, rinsing again even though she didn't need to, and then she finally exited, toweled off, and headed over to the lockers just as Chung came in. The woman nodded, walked past her, and started changing right where Roy was finishing getting dressed.

Two seconds later, Roy came around the side, pulling his shirt on over his head. Shrina had her top and panties on, but this time didn't make anything of it.

"I was thinking," Roy said. "When briefing's over today, I'd love to hear more about what happened. It's fascinating how a corporation could gain so much power and then fall. Whaddaya say?"

She nodded. "Yeah, yeah. Okay."

It was a story she hadn't wanted to tell much right after it happened when all of it had been so fresh. Now, though, she was fine with it. And maybe… maybe she'd liked what she'd seen, even though she wasn't supposed to be looking, and was curious about what kind of guy he was. He was in damn good shape, but then again, they all were. They wouldn't have been chosen otherwise.

He gave her a smile and moved on, and she glanced down to realize that she still wasn't wearing pants. How embarrassing.

When she marched back out, the others had gathered and were watching clips of their runs through the course. She caught a glimpse of Roy's that showed him scaling the wall faster than seemed possible, then narrowly dodging the simulated attacks thrown at him—similar to how a tennis ball or baseball machine operated. Whatever he may lack in fighting ability, he certainly made up for with his moves.

She glanced over at him, impressed, and he grinned.

When hers came up, she couldn't help analyzing each move with scrutiny. Here she was among the best simply because of her role in the takedown of New Origins, and she was, in her opinion, moving quite sloppily. Even Chung was moving better than she had, and that lady was the runt of the litter.

Richards entered and Shrina braced for the worst, knowing she might have screwed things up for herself and maybe even the team. Or maybe the team had already fallen apart with what had happened to Drakes and now the news was going to drop.

All of it would be over—her training and enhancements pointless. She glanced at Roy for comfort but instead saw a flash of that image from before, of him standing there naked. Oh, God, she couldn't get it out of her head now. When he turned toward her, he blushed and quickly turned away.

Was he having the same thoughts? She had to believe he was. With a deep breath, she reminded herself to be a professional. They were all warriors now, effectively vampire hunters. There was no room for this silliness.

"So, how'd they like us?" Chung asked.

"Doesn't matter," Richards replied, pulling up his

wrist computer and swiping over to the screens. A world map appeared.

"How's that?" Chung said and looked from the map to him, confused. "I have a feeling I should shut up and wait for you to tell me."

He gave her a half-humored grin, but he was clearly focused. Somber. "We tracked 'em down. There was another attack, this time in Tunis."

"North Africa?" Shrina asked.

"That'd be where it is, yes. Capital of Tunisia. Satellites picked them up during an attack on a local militia group and tracked them to where we can assume their hideout is. Tunisian authorities have been asked to be on standby and have the place surrounded. Guess who's going international, ASAP."

Reactions were mixed, but Shrina felt a rush of excitement. She'd figured they would be in training for months or at least weeks. Moving out this fast and getting the chance to see action right away meant no opportunities for her to sit around and think the worst, waiting for the next time the enemy would strike.

No, they were bringing the fight to them.

Whatever fantasies she was having about Roy would have to wait, but maybe that was for the best. She thought of Trent up there in space and realized it was best if she focused on the job, at least until they had more answers about his situation.

"So, it's too late to back out," Richards said, "but I'll ask anyway. Is anyone having cold feet?"

"Hell no," Chung shouted, and the others agreed.

"Well then," Richards said with a grin and motioned for them to follow. "Let's get suited up and hit the jets. It's go time, ladies and gents."

"I'm going to kill me some vamps," one of the guys said—a tall one whose name Shrina hadn't caught yet.

"String their fangs on a necklace," Chung replied. "We'll see who'll get more."

"You're on, crouton," he said, and Shrina worried she wasn't going to like him, whatever his name was.

Three other guys brushed past, clearly old Navy SEAL types with their shades and caps, likely part of the contingent of contractors sent over to join the team of enhanced soldiers. Shrina glanced around at the rest of the team—about twenty in all—wondering who she'd most trust to have her back. A large African-American man gave her a nod, and two Marines were making fun of the fact that the enemy was being referred to as vampires. Others were walking at their own pace, assessing each other just as she was, but they were being a tad less obvious about it.

She made a note of watching without letting on that she was watching and decided to hold off forming opinions just yet. When she turned back, Roy was at her side.

"I'll get us in close," he said. "You take them out. Deal?"

Shrina grinned. "You were watching?"

"Hey, I was waiting for you at the end because I finished first. Honestly, it was a long wait."

"Screw you."

"I'm just saying you could use some pointers."

"Oh?" she said and turned to him, frowning. "And you'd be the one to give them?"

"If you'll show me how to fight like that," he said, rubbing his chest where she'd hit him.

"It doesn't still hurt," she said, rolling her eyes. "If we can heal from a knife wound, I'm sure that didn't leave a bruise."

"The memory of it did," he replied. "So… deal?"

She nodded. "Sure, deal."

"It's a date then, a kill-vampires-together date."

"I never said—" she started to say but didn't have time to finish the thought because just then Richards shouted for everyone to shut up.

He held a hand to his ear and said, "Repeat." Everyone stood frozen while his face went pale. "Roger that. On our way."

When he looked up at them, his eyes were narrowed. "Forget Tunisia, for now. Those bloodsuckers are out on the streets right now, a secondary attack on the launch site. Apparently, they're trying hard to make a move on the gateway. We're going to stop them."

"Anybody ever stop to think," one of the SEALs said, "that maybe opening that gateway let something in?"

"Damn," Chung replied, looking thoughtful.

"I don't care two shits for your theories," Richards said, "not right now. Right now we need to shoot first and ask questions later. Go!"

They all charged out, Shrina feeling a whole new rush. The previous attack hadn't been a one-off. Not only was the enemy international, but they were making new moves, striking in specific locations. It sounded like their goal was to get weapons into Tunisia or maybe to hijack space travel at the launch site. She'd assumed it was about disrupting the launch—maybe a terrorist strike—but now she was thinking it was part of something bigger.

Being on the front line of uncovering that "something" and being able to kill some of those bastards in the process really made her day.

12

TRENT: UNKNOWN PLANET B

Trent had no idea how long he'd been running but kept on. Each breath filled him with more energy and caused him to forget the pain he'd been in not long before. He crashed through the bushes, not worrying about scratches or potential poisons or other issues that could arise since he had the protection of his armor. He was close enough to see the details of the ship now, pausing when he saw that the ship was on the edge of a cliff. It wasn't about to fall off as his pod had done, but getting to it would be tricky.

Or it might have been tricky for someone who didn't have thrusters in their boots. He positioned himself and set the thrusters to "on," only to find himself pushed up and sideways, banging into a nearby tree. The ground came up fast and he landed with a thud. Head spinning, he sat there for a moment. The previous crash, or possibly the use of his thrusters when the pod had crashed the second time, must have broken them. He pushed himself up, considering other options for getting up to the ledge.

The exoskeleton helped with strength so he could jump higher than normal, but this was a bigger jump than he was capable of even with the help. Gravity felt slightly off, but not enough to make a real difference.

Climbing was the only option. Getting a foothold with his armor on was harder than Trent would have thought. If anything, it was a hindrance, but he wasn't about to leave his armor behind—not on some unknown planet and especially not after having seen those red eyes.

As he climbed, he contemplated what those eyes could have been. An illusion? Some sort of a giant demon, maybe, and he was actually dead? He doubted that part, but didn't want to rule anything out. The most likely answer was that some attacking alien force had some sort of image-projection gimmick that they used to scare the hell out of their enemies.

If so, it had certainly worked.

Trent grabbed hold of the rocky ledge above and

leaped the last bit to the edge, gaining his footing. Landing in a crouch, his first instinct was to make a beeline for the cockpit and check on survivors. But when the leaves of the dense jungle to his left rustled, he had to reevaluate that instinct. He hadn't run into any alien life force out here yet, but that certainly didn't mean there wasn't one.

And he had a feeling he was about to meet it now.

Whatever he did, he told himself to stay calm and be prepared. But when he reached over his back, he realized he hadn't even thought to grab his rifle in all the chaos. The Ka-Bar knife was also back in the pod, which meant he had no weapons.

When the leaves moved again and something appeared, running straight at him, he decided there was only one possible move—to sprint to the ship. A quick glance back showed three creatures no taller than his knees that looked like a cross between a wolf and a movie depiction of a small dinosaur. They alternated between running on all fours and rising up onto their hind legs while slashing out with large claws. He was almost at the ship when the first one reached him, and he heard a scraping sound as its claws hit the metal of his suit.

"Open the fuck up!" he shouted and was relieved to see the AI from his suit sync with the ship and open the side door. With a leap he was in and the door was closing behind him. One of those little bastards jumped in to join him, but Trent spun, knowing exactly where the extra rifles were stored, and snatched one down.

The creature was on his suit, almost to his head. Trent spun, slammed the helmet back on, and threw himself at the nearby wall. When he turned, the little bastard had just landed on the floor and was looking up at him with beady little green eyes, preparing to leap again. As it did, he brought the rifle down and scorched the little shit.

Apparently, these aliens weren't invincible, especially not to Marine-Corps-issued blasters or rifles.

More scraping sounded from outside the ship, moving to the top, and he spun with his rifle aimed, just in case. When nothing else happened, he relaxed and opened his faceplate again. The stench of the dead alien hit his nostrils like skunk mixed with burnt bacon, so he put the faceplate back in place and cleared the air from his suit.

A horrible thought hit him. With all that noise and no response, it was unlikely anyone aboard was alive.

Heart pounding, he made his way to the cockpit and froze. A leg was visible in the entryway, and when he passed, he was able to see a puddle of blood. Next, he came to the cockpit where Captain

Aarol stared up at the ceiling with a blank, dead gaze.

Seeing him here, Trent's gut clenched. It was horrible to see the man dead, but worse than that, Aarol had been assigned to fly with Enise. Trent turned to the next seat with great trepidation and froze when he saw no helmet, just a bun of blonde hair and her head pressed up against the bulkhead. There was nothing he wanted to see less than that same dead look in her eyes, but he had to know.

"Enise," he said, hoping beyond hope. He stepped forward, pulling his helmet off completely as he did so.

Her eyes were closed. How many times had he lain with her back at the space station, staring into her face as she slept after an intimate evening? It was where they'd met at a duty station before being allowed to test for Space Fleet Marines. Back then, he'd almost started to imagine he would grow old with her, maybe raise a family together. She was the only woman he'd felt that way about other than Shrina. What had begun as a fling, a rebound, had started to change within him, to melt his heart. Then had come the day when she told him she had no intention of ever raising a family. She said she meant to give her life to the Marines and dedicate herself to space exploration, ensuring that the people of Earth had other planets to expand into. He had laughed at the irony because he had broken it off with Shrina, stating very similar reasons. He knew he deserved to have it thrown back in his face.

The whole discussion had been infuriating, and when he'd asked where that left them, she had reached down, taken him in her hands, and said that they were exactly where they were meant to be.

"What the hell's that supposed to mean?" he'd said, not wanting to lose his temper in the face of the ecstasy of her touch.

"Means we can do this every chance we get," she had replied, moving herself onto him, her breath warm on his neck. "Means we work hard out there, then play hard in here."

He still hated himself for what had come next, but he eventually pushed her off and turned away from her, shaking his head as he said, "No."

"No? I don't understand."

He had stood up, found his clothes, and begun to dress as he replied, "Means that's not enough for me. When you're ready for a grownup relationship, you know where to find me."

Then he'd left and it was over. Every night he'd waited. Every time he passed her in the halls or at training, he glanced over, hoping to see a change in her expression. But none had come.

And now… this. He pulled off his helmet and bowed his head, about to close his eyes when—

A flutter of her eyelids startled him and he fell back, pressed up against Aarol's corpse. Enise was looking up at him, her dazed expression melting into a mixture of relief and worry.

"You… how?" she asked and then coughed up blood.

"Stay with me," he said, knowing what that cough meant. He knelt at her side, searching for the wound, and then found it. Her armor had been bent in the collision, he imagined, because now it was pressing into her, more than her body could handle. Apparently, it wasn't as protective as they liked to believe.

"Where… are the others?" she asked, unable to move her head, but her eyes rolled to follow him as he stood and backed away.

"Mercer never made it," she groaned, her breaths heavy with the effort of speaking.

The situation took him a moment to process, but then he was at her side again. He shook off the armored gloves so he could hold her face in his hands.

"I'm sorry to hear it," he said. "But... they're gone. Everyone's gone."

"We saw the escape pod… from the other ship. I thought it might be you, so I made Aarol follow, even though this wasn't the destination." She bit her lip, moist eyes glimmering. "You… don't give up."

"And you either!" he demanded, kissing her forehead. "I… I never stopped caring for you."

She smiled at that, the type of smile someone gives right before they fall asleep, except she was never going to wake from this sleep.

"I loved you, you know," she replied. "In my own way… and still do."

She coughed once more, breathed heavily, and then was gone. Dead. Leaving him to shout and hold her close, then punch the control panel with all his might. He'd forgotten that he wasn't wearing gloves and instantly regretted the outburst. Pulling his hand back, he held it tight, biting his knuckle against the pain—both physical, though that would heal fairly fast with his enhancements, and to keep himself from losing it emotionally.

Shit, he was a Marine, a Space Fleet Marine no less, the best of the best. He wasn't about to go all emotional on some alien planet. He'd just discovered a habitable environment—the Holy Grail, basically. Unless he got that information back home, it would mean the others had all died for nothing.

With all of this in mind, he pulled himself together, closed Enise's eyes, and put his helmet and gloves back on. He returned to the rear room and found the other two members of the flight team slumped over in their seats with blood dripping down their faces. The hollow look in the eyes of one of them showed that he was dead, but the other man was staring at him, eyes wide.

"Helms, is that you?" the man said. "My… my legs."

Trent ran over, checking the man and cringing at the sight of part of the ship that had broken off and was sticking into the man's right thigh. A puddle of blood was forming out of the man's sight. "Stan, right? Stanley Ortiz?"

The man nodded.

"Stan, I'm going to get you out of here. Just stay put."

"Where're you going?"

Trent looked to the windows, considering his options. "I'm going to see if I can find other survivors or a comms device that works. Get you out of here."

"Don't leave me," Stan pleaded.

After a moment's consideration, Trent nodded. "Okay, buddy. Let's see what we can do here."

His first move was to find the ship's first aid kit. He found the morphine and shot it into Stan. Next came the tissue gun.

"Get ready. This'll hurt like hell," he said and then

pulled Stan's leg free from the ship. Stan screamed with pain as blood spurted from his wound, but Trent was ready. He jammed the tissue gun into the opening and pulled the trigger, filling the wound. The bleeding stopped immediately. It would swell and possibly become infected, but he wouldn't die from it on that day.

Just one more reason to hurry up and get them out of this place.

As Stan sat back, controlling his breathing and letting the morphine kick in, Trent moved around the ship, preparing to take off. He checked the equipment but got nothing out of it. The ship had apparently been destroyed in the fall and was useless. Next, he considered other options. There was the beacon others would be able to use to find them, but who knew how long that could take? If he could find other ships intact, he could try to fly out of there or at least send a proper message home. Not knowing how to fly made that prospect less likely, but he at least knew enough about the process to give it a try. And while exploring, he figured he might be able to learn more about the planet.

His first move was to stock up on supplies. Food and water were priorities, but he also strapped on two blaster pistols, the rifle, a Ka-Bar knife, and he even found an old-school rifle that used actual bullets. Then he had an idea—his own thrusters were fried, but it was likely Aarol's weren't. He spent a few minutes switching them out and then steeled his nerves, glancing through the front display at the jungle ahead of him.

He had no idea what he could get into out there, but he'd have to try.

13

ESPINOZA: SPACE, UNKNOWN PLANET A

Finally, the storm had died down and the sky was clear. Espinoza had just finished putting his armor back on and was still feeling the thrill of being with Kim. It had been wild and unexpected. Perfect.

A glance back showed her slipping into her uniform, her perfect breasts now covered with her sports bra. That, too, was about to become covered, and she met his gaze with a chuckle.

"You trying to sneak another peek?"

"Might not see them again for a while once we're back with the others," he admitted. "I have to ensure my memory of them is solid."

She grinned, dropped her uniform and pulled up the sports bra, flashing him right there.

"Corporal!" a voice behind Espinoza shouted,

and Kim's expression became horror-stricken as she quickly covered herself up.

Espinoza turned to see one of the sergeants—Belmes, his HUD showed. The guy pulled up his faceplate, frowning.

"I've been looking all over for you two," he said, "and it turns out you're off in some cave playing I'll-show-you-mine-if-you-show-me-yours."

"You're just mad because you didn't get an invite," she countered, turning to finish putting on her uniform, then her armor.

"You had us seriously worried," Belmes said. "Half the team wanted to go out looking for you in the storm. The other half assumed you were dead."

"Thanks for believing in us," Espinoza said.

He scoffed. "Hell, no. I was one of the first to proclaim you dead. I'm only here because Gunny forced us to go on patrols. Lucky me, I found you and got a peep show at the same time. Though probably nothing as good as Espinoza here, am I right?"

He walked up to Espinoza, eyebrows raised as if waiting for the details. When he saw Espinoza frowning and not giving anything up, he scoffed and turned to get out of there.

"Probably still a virgin," he added. "Both of you, hurry your asses so we can report in. I need to hit the head, bad."

Espinoza glanced over to the corner they'd designated as their own little piss spot during the storm, the same corner Belmes was about to step through. A glance at Kim showed him she wasn't about to say anything, so neither did Espinoza.

Belmes stopped, sniffed, and glanced back. "Both of you need to shower. You smell like hell."

He walked out and the two cracked up, both covering their mouths and trying not to let him hear or think they were mocking him. Maybe it was the giddiness of being alive and saved or the thrill of having gotten laid—he wasn't sure—but each step outside came with a bounce, even in the heavy armor.

His smile faded when he saw the devastation of the storm. Large piles of dirt formed zigzagging patterns in the earth. Many trees had been toppled, and it almost looked like a different planet.

"They were totally screwing," Belmes was telling Franco, who turned to see Espinoza, offering a huge thumbs up.

"Guys, maybe we don't turn it into the campfire chat topic?" Espinoza said.

"Oh, damn," Franco said and looked at him, then back to Belmes. "Because he doesn't want the gunny to know."

"Wait, what?" Belmes asked.

Espinoza tried to signal Franco to shut up, not even sure how he knew there was anything there. When Franco spilled the beans about the kiss, however, the easy assumption was that he had seen it.

"My man," Belmes said, though not hiding the hint of jealousy in his eyes. "How does he do it?"

"Maybe you gotta have a sexy name like Espinoza," Franco said with a shrug. "Hell, I'd probably do him if he whispered his name in my ear, softly."

"Shut up," Espinoza said, hitting him. "Seriously, both of you, focus on the mission and not where my lips or other parts of me go."

"Hey, like someone said when we landed," Franco said, hands up in surrender, "it might be up to us to populate this place, you know? That means—"

Espinoza tuned him out, realizing that, like an idiot, he'd completely forgotten about protection the night before. Damn. He could very much become the first dad on an alien planet. That tripped him out, so no matter what the others were rambling on about, he just stared out at the skies, trying to figure out how they'd handle that. It wasn't like they had baby spacesuits or anything, though if they stayed on planet forever, they wouldn't need one. Then again, could he live with her for the rest of his life? That idea was scary in itself.

"You boys done talking about me and Espi here doing it?" Kim asked, exiting the cave. In all her armor, faceplate down, she was just another one of the guys. A Marine. But damn, the sight of her in that cave would stick with him for some time.

Her question received a couple of chuckles, but no comment.

All four started heading back, and Espinoza quickly learned something about Kim. As much as he was a gentleman and didn't talk, she was the opposite. She started telling them about how he'd taken her in his arms up against that cold, stone wall, and he had to interject.

"Kim... really?"

She shrugged. "Why have secrets here? We could all die tomorrow and you'd want the legend of your sex-ventures to be lost from the annals of history?"

"No, did you—" Franco looked at Espinoza with wide eyes. "Ana—"

"No!" Espinoza shouted and stormed off. He wasn't sure why it mattered. It just felt like high school locker room B.S. and not an appropriate topic of Marine chatter on an alien planet.

After a minute, Kim jogged up next to him.

"Sorry. I didn't know it meant so much to you,"

she said. "It was just fun, I thought. And… I don't know. Most guys I've been with don't mind talking about it with their friends, so I started doing it, too."

"Yeah, well, not me."

"What? The talking part or it just being fun?" she asked, now looking more interested.

"I don't know, okay?" He laughed. "Hell, maybe I just need a beer, I don't know. Did you even tell them about the vampires that attacked, or were you too busy describing the contours of my dick?"

"To be fair, she didn't get to that, and we wouldn't want to hear it," Franco said.

"Shut up," they both replied.

"Yeah, shut up," Belmes added, jogging up to them. "What's this about vampires?"

They told him and Franco, and both held their rifles up, more alert.

"Probably should have led with that," Franco stated. "I mean, honestly that *does* have more to do with our chance of survival than you two screwing like bunnies."

"Right, my mistake," Kim said.

Belmes recommended they pick up the pace, leading them back to the ship. Once they'd arrived, Kim and Espinoza filled in the gunny and captain, others leaning in with interest.

"So, we're not alone out here," Ellins said, thoughtfully.

"We'll have to be smarter about patrols," the captain added. "Double up guard duty."

"Yes, sir," Ellins replied. "But… we also might want to try and figure out where they are. We don't want to be sitting ducks here, waiting for them to attack. Maybe it wouldn't be a big deal if the ship was intact, but it's not."

"Smart," the captain admitted, "but risky. And based on that storm, we don't want to get too spread out." He glanced around. "If we set a team of four on it, would that work?"

"Good number to scout it out and provide backup. Get in, see what we're dealing with, and report back." She scanned the Marines and said, "Me, Espinoza, Kim, and… Franco."

"Good to go, Gunny," the captain said, but then thought about it. "Kim, the comms are fried, aren't they?"

She nodded.

"If there's another ship out there, see if you can get some intel on comms—what they have and whether it works."

"Yes, sir."

With a nod, he headed back to the others.

"So, team," Ellins said, "think we can handle this?"

They all answered in the affirmative, though Espinoza was already trying to avoid eye contact with both Ellins and Kim, not sure how to feel about the situation. Awkward was a major understatement.

After a quick meal and sharing stories with some of the group, they set off on their way to hunt down some space vampires.

14

SHRINA: EARTH, KENNEDY SPACE CENTER

Arriving at the Kennedy Space Center so soon after taking off was a thrill, especially since it didn't allow much time for the adrenaline rush to die down. As soon as they landed, Richards was at the door with the stairs in place, checking everyone on their way out.

"Make 'em pay," Richards told Shrina when she was up, then gave her a slap on the helmet.

She wasn't sure if he was saying that to everyone or if he knew something about her past with Trent. Either way, she meant to kick some vampire ass.

"Where're they at?" someone ahead of her shouted, though she couldn't be sure who in the mixture of darkness and bright lights.

A Marine joined them as they ran, saying, "We've

been going back and forth with them on the landing zone. Right now we have them pinned down but—"

BRRRT! BRRRT!

Shots hit, tearing through the Marine. Return fire opened up and Shrina dove for cover, trying to get a handle on where the shots had come from. At least now she knew these bastards weren't mere vampires. They were shooting at her and her allies, which meant they had some sense about them. At least they weren't completely crazed, not all like the ones she'd encountered when rescuing her sister.

Richards directed them into teams, but halfway through his orders all hell broke loose and they had to figure it out as they went. A team of vampires came at them, some shooting while others moved to flank them, but Shrina and Roy broke off in one direction to meet the enemy halfway with a couple of others. The SEALs ran in another direction.

Moving along in the darkness, they found cover, shot, and then advanced to the next cover, which forced the vampires to slow their advance. Chung shouted through her comms that she was hit and that her armor had been pierced, but moments later she was at it again, pushing through the pain. If it wasn't lethal, her enhancements would help her heal from it.

The fight moved over to the hangar on the east side, and at least two vampires had fallen.

Shrina turned a corner to find a vampire with his back to her, aimed in on Marines taking cover to her left. Two shots to the back of the head and he was down. Another one appeared, turning her way and firing, and she ducked back and around the other side, sprinting to reach the opposite end of the building and come around that way.

Roy joined her there, and when he saw what she was doing, he said, "I'll cover you from above."

He ran for the side of the building, jumped, and scrambled up its side. She reached the edge of the building and prepared, clutching her rifle, and then stepped out into a group of three vampires moving her way to catch them by surprise.

Several more were past them, fleeing—not in retreat, she realized, but making a move for one of those spaceships!

Shrina charged in, determined not to let them get another of those ships. If Trent was up there, she was damn sure not going to let these monsters have a chance of finding him before Earth mounted another mission.

"You're insane!" Roy said, leaping up to follow. "I love it!"

"Love this," she shouted over her shoulder and

then leaped up onto the loading equipment, sending a four-round burst into the back and head of one of the vampires. She then jumped off and charged, drawing her Ka-Bar. A vampire appeared from her left, mowed down a second later by shots from Roy, while other shots went off from both directions—friendly and enemy fire both equally likely to hit her.

But she continued her charge.

The closest vampire turned to see her coming, eyes red, with veins on his neck and forehead to match. He wore body armor not so different from hers except without the helmet. When he came at her, though, with fangs bared and claws extending from his hands, the idea that these things could be actual vampires didn't seem so farfetched.

But even that thought didn't faze her. She let out another burst from her rifle, wild and one-handed, and then she was on him. She used the rifle grip to swing the weapon around like a baton along her arm, slicing for his neck with her knife.

Two of Roy's shots joined the barrage, and the vampire stumbled back, staring at her. Others came to their comrade's rescue, leaping over the craft and crawling at her like the beasts they were. Then, one flew through the air, knocking Shrina back to the ground. Her blade made contact, thrust up into his skull from the throat during impact, but now she was under him and others were coming at her, trying to get in a good bite or a slash of their claws, and attempting to rip off her helmet.

There were more shots and then the clang of a rifle hitting either Roy or Chung, who were fighting them off, or doing their best. It was enough for Shrina to roll the dead vampire off of her and join in the fight. A large one was there, one eye scarred but his good one watching as his comrades fell, and he cursed. At the sound of his voice, she realized it was the one she'd hit with the arc rod at the apartment parking garage, apparently healed.

"You," he said, voice heavy with hatred. "You."

She ran for him, but when he glanced around and saw he was the only one still standing, he took off in retreat. She followed, charging across the asphalt. When he leaped up and hit the top of the fence, using it as leverage to throw himself off into the night, she did her best to follow but hit the side of the fence instead. She pulled herself up and jumped off to the other side, running.

But there was no sight of him.

A thud sounded behind her and she spun for the attack, only to see Roy. He held up her rifle and tossed it to her. "Dropped this back there."

"Did I?" she said as she caught it and slung it over her shoulder. In the chaos, she hadn't even thought of it. She'd just wanted to catch that vampire. Something about him spoke of power—the kind that meant he might be a leader. If she *had* caught up to him without her weapon, would she have made it very far?

"No sign of him, I'm guessing," Roy said, eyes roving through the darkness.

"The way he moved..." She shook her head, amazed. "They're better than us."

"Than you, anyway," Roy replied with a grin.

She shrugged. "You could clear the fence the way he did?"

"I honestly didn't see. I was busy fighting off the other two that tried to chase you down when you went running after him."

Now that he mentioned it, his armor was splattered with blood. Nodding at the blood, she asked, "Theirs?"

"Yeah. Thinking we can do tests on it?"

"That or the corpses," she said, noticing that the sounds of fighting had stopped. What the Marines hadn't been able to do, she and her team had managed in no time at all.

"One's not a corpse," he replied, grinning. "They caught a live one."

"No shit?"

He motioned her back and they jogged to the

fence, quickly scaled it, and found the team surrounded by Marines. In their midst was a restrained vampire.

"What now?" Shrina asked Richards when she saw him standing on the opposite side of the circle.

"Teams are to stand guard and be ready for more hits. But mostly," he said and paused to look at the members of his team, checking to see if they were all still there, "the real hunt begins."

15

TRENT: UNKNOWN PLANET B

"How you holding up, Stan?" Trent asked, putting his helmet back on before going outside.

He'd been treating Stan's wound, hoping to make his move at the right time. After a last look at their surroundings, he moved for the rear of the ship. Once there, he listened for any sounds from outside and considered where they should start. If they could make it to the top of the cliffs where the waterfall originated, they could get a damn good view of this place.

"Stan?" He glanced back to see Stan undoing his harness and trying to stand. The man nearly fell over, so Trent darted back over to grab him. With a hand around him to help him move, he said, "Rely on the exoskeleton in the suit. Try not to put any excess pressure on the wound."

"Roger that," Stan said, leaning with one hand at the side of the doorway.

With a few whispers of "shit, shit, shit," Trent nodded and opened the door. He took a deep breath to calm his nerves, and then they ran for it.

The moment of regret came almost immediately as those damn raptor aliens appeared—one leaping from a tree and two more darting out of the bushes. They moved for Stan, as if sensing his weakness. Trent pulled out his blasters and turned them into fricassee, but not before one had latched onto Stan's faceplate, angrily trying to pull it free. As Trent blasted it in half, Stan took a step back. With a shriek of terror, Stan realized that his last step had taken him over the side of the hill, and he was falling.

"Thrusters!" Trent called out, but even as the words left his mouth, he knew it was too late. Before the man could react, he hit one of the rocks that was sticking out, toppled over, and landed headfirst. His neck snapped, the impact killing him instantly.

Trent cursed, kicking open air, and turned with blasters raised, searching for more of them to kill, *hoping* for more of them to kill. But there weren't any so he ran, having decided it was better to move on before more predators arrived no matter how badly he wanted revenge.

It was a relief to find that his thrusters worked, and he immediately used them to reach the next ledge. Even though the thrusters gave out momentarily, he landed smoothly and broke into a run, finding a part of the hill that led up and into a steep incline where tall trees and large leaves blocked out the sky and the orange light that glowed across it all.

Dammit, how could that have happened to Stan? The guy had often been a jerk back in training, always the one to try and towel-snap the other guys' sacks in the showers and stupid stuff like that, but on the field? When it came to training and killing, he had many times performed with the best of them, never letting a teammate down. If Stan hadn't made it, Trent wondered what chances someone like himself had. But he pushed on, refusing to let those thoughts wear him down. People had died; that was that, and he needed to focus on the next move. One step at a time.

When he came to a clearing and paused to catch his breath, he took a moment to marvel at the way the sky seemed permanently stuck in that orange hue. Although appearing almost like a dot in the sky, the small sun was apparently enough to keep all of this vegetation alive.

A leaf moved and he cursed, wishing he had more time to keep still but knowing that he had to keep moving. Even before he had taken his third step, however, those creatures were on his trail again, ducking in and out of the path he had created, and leaping from tree to tree. Up ahead, he spotted the cave he'd been heading toward. There was a large opening back behind the foliage and overgrowth, and when he turned to the other hills he imagined that the dark spots on those hills might also be caves.

He had an option here—turn and fight the little bastards, hoping their claws didn't stand a chance against his armor, or escape into the cave. Part of him thought the idea of running into the cave might be suicide, cornering himself like that. And even worse, what if the caves were where those things lived and he was simply throwing himself on their mercy? The Marine in him, however, said it would be good to have a wall to his back so they couldn't surround him. One thing Trent had learned about himself early on in his adult life was that the Marine always won.

He turned away from the hillside, leaped for the cave, and plunged into the darkness within. Once he was in, however, he saw that it wasn't pure darkness. A strange, yellow glow emanated from deep inside the cave. He stood there, looking between the darkness and the glow, and only then realized something else—the creatures hadn't followed him in. In fact, a glance back outside showed leaves rustling as they retreated.

Odd, he thought as he turned back into the cave, but that thought didn't last long as a movement in the darkness vanished the glow, followed by two monstrous red eyes.

Instinct told him to run, but his body told him to piss himself. He listened to the former, fighting his body and instead telling it to move his fucking legs. All he could do was throw himself backwards into the sunlight, only to find himself tumbling down the hillside. Suddenly, the ground was gone and he was falling. As his mind raced for options among images of Enise and her dented armor, he pushed his legs up in front of him toward a bit of a cliff to his left and turned on his thrusters. He was thrown in the opposite direction, and he wrapped his arm around the nearest tree trunk, spun around it, and placed himself on an unsteady clump of dirt.

And then his heart stopped because he saw what it was that had frightened him—the owner of the red eyes. Its long, leathery wings were spread wide, and the orange light shined through the wings so that they glowed. The beast turned to take him in.

He'd seen images similar to this one back home

in fantasy movies. The closest description he could come up with was that of a dragon, with its long neck and tail, horned head and teeth as long as swords. Scratch that—it wasn't just a description or a comparison. These things *were* dragons.

His head spun with the thought that the fleet had been taken out by dragons. He scrunched his nose, considering how insane it sounded, even in his own head. How the hell could dragons take out fully armored, shielded space fighters?

The dragon didn't give him much time to contemplate it, however. Already spreading its wings, it let out a roar that shook the hillside, then turned to him with its red eyes and opened its mouth wide. Flames rose up from inside the beast's throat, then shot out.

Trent didn't intend to be there when those flames connected. He was pretty sure that if dragons *had* been what had taken out the fleet, his armor wouldn't stand a chance. His only option, therefore, seemed to be to lunge sideways and into another one of those caves.

He turned on his thrusters to give him a head start, hoping they'd stay on this time. He landed in an all-out sprint. Even though the exoskeleton could certainly make him run fast, he was pretty damn sure the dragon would be able to move faster still, so he had to come up with a plan, and quickly.

A golden glow came from deep within this cave as well, enough for him to see small passageways breaking off from the main chamber. Since the light from the entrance was blocked by what he imagined was the dragon, Trent threw himself into one of those side passages and ran. He hoped the fire wouldn't follow him into the passage and catch him. He didn't want to die. If he died, then Enise's death and that of all the others would have been pointless.

The passage didn't take him far before turning back toward the main cavern, but there were other tunnels, ledges and more. *A Marine could get lost in here,* he thought, but he knew he needed to keep moving.

A roar sounded, then other roars in reply. He cursed, realizing that his worst fears were coming true—he had suspected the caverns would be full of dragons, possibly thousands of them, but hearing them made it very real.

He turned left and crawled into an opening, horrified at the thought of the rocks caving in on him and being stuck there, left to die in the armor that would become his casket. But to his relief, the tunnel opened into another cavern, and there the glow was stronger

—strong enough that he was able to see that the floor was oddly shaped, like a series of mounds, or... *Shit,* he realized as he thought it, *these are eggs. Dragon eggs!*

His eyes rose to the ceiling above—a rock cave covered in stalactites. But it wasn't only stalactites up there. There were thousands of what appeared to be sleeping dragons. They were hanging like bats.

And then one of them opened its red, glowing eyes, spread its wings, and came for him.

Trent turned and dove back the way he'd come. He belly-crawled through the tunnel, escaping just in time to avoid the explosive flames at his back. Rolling to the right, he found another passage, this one leading back out to the light—the natural orange, glowing light.

He ran for it, entering a larger chamber in the process. A second dragon appeared at his side and roared. It dove as he leaped with thrusters on, making it into the opening. He had somehow gone full circle, it seemed, because when he landed, he landed right on the wing of Enise's ship.

The dragon emerged behind him and he had just enough time to see that it was much smaller than the first—a baby, perhaps? Not that it really mattered since it was still trying to kill him.

He ran along the wing of the ship, slipping over to the side as the dragon nearly caught him in its teeth. He then slid under the wing and sprang down to the ground on the other side. The dragon tried to follow but hit the side of the ship and knocked it loose in the process.

Trent spun, gasping in shock as he watched both dragon and ship, interlocked, fall over the side of the hill. He ran to the edge and watched the two thud through trees and then come to a stop at the bottom. While most would have turned and run again at this point, a small whimper from below drew his attention.

It sounded nothing like a dragon. More like… a child? He frowned, hating himself for this decision, and made his way down the hill. When he reached the ship, he proceeded with caution until he could see the dragon. It was still there, but it looked like its wing was pinned down by the ship. Its head turned to face him, and he was interested to see that not only had the glowing red left its eyes, but he could almost see a human side to it. Wide, worried eyes stared at him, scared yet hopeful, and it whimpered again. That noise had definitely come from the dragon.

With a glance around for the mother, Trent approached. "I'm not going to hurt you," he said, not even sure why he was speaking to it. "We didn't come to attack you. I promise."

The small dragon looked at him and whimpered again, then set its head down on the grass.

"I don't know why the hell I'm acting like you understand me," he said, "but if I help you out of this, can you not eat me?"

The dragon actually lifted its head and seemed to nod.

Very carefully, Trent approached the dragon. When he was close, he reached up and removed his helmet to show he meant no threat and that he wasn't scary. The effect was surprising. Immediately, the dragon seemed to calm. It lowered its head as if bowing, and then waited for him. He approached cautiously, aware that at any moment this beast could snap out and bite his head clean off, likely swallowing it in a single gulp.

So far, so good.

He made his way to the dragon's side, amazed at the way its scales seemed to glimmer, almost changing colors like a rainbow in a stream. It had spikes along its back, but they were elegant and flowing as if they were part of a blown-glass creation, a majestic work of art.

As he approached, he saw the wing trapped by the edge of his ship, as he had suspected.

"I got you," he said and then bent at the knees, putting all of his leverage into a giant shove, boosters and all, and the exoskeleton gave him the support he needed. "Hmmphh," he groaned as he pushed, but the ship just barely budged. Again he braced himself, this time yelling at the top of his lungs as he pushed.

"AHHHHHHHH!"

Suddenly, the young dragon was free and the ship was moving, only…it wasn't just him. He'd been helped by a larger dragon. Massive wings beat as its head lowered, and then it turned its eyes toward him.

Trent saw himself in those eyes, but then he saw another form shaped like a golden, glowing woman. He cocked his head, confused, heart thudding in his chest so that it seemed to send shockwaves through his body and blood coursing through his skull.

The large dragon broke eye contact and nudged the smaller dragon. Then, heads pressed together, a golden glow emanated from the larger one that he guessed must be the mother. When the dragon turned back to him, a calm feeling spread out from her, along with the word *Come*. The word wasn't spoken as much as it just came over him, and he wanted to go.

The mother dragon led the other, and he climbed with them until they reached another of those caves. At that point, Trent had to pause and ask himself what the hell he was thinking. Was he really about to follow two dragons back into the caves—caves where he had just seen many more dragons sleeping? Glancing back over his shoulder, he looked out to see the waterfall, the large mountains, and towering ice structures spread before him, and he felt at peace again.

Perhaps he would be found if he waited out there. He could hunt and stay out of the dragons' way. But he would always wonder… *what if*.

So he took the first step into the cave and then another. Soon he was in darkness, but the golden glow had lit up again, bobbing ahead, so he knew that must be where the two dragons had gone.

He followed them deeper and deeper into the cave. Soon he found himself in a cavern that was unlike anything he'd ever seen before. Jagged purple rocks lined the walls, intermittently replaced by smooth blue ones that held a gentle glow to them. The light cast by that gentle glow was enough to see that the cave opened into a massive cavern. His heart skipped a beat and he held his breath at the sight of the dragons, or rather the spot where they should have been. Instead of the dragons, he now saw the faint outlines of what looked like humans. He picked up the pace, trying to close the distance. Now he could see that they weren't just humans, but a mother and daughter, perhaps, with the glow highlighting them. They were stepping into a pool of water, and as their feet touched it, their glow intensified. A warmth filled the cavern and Trent could almost hear a song coming from somewhere, though when he strained his ears to hear, he wasn't sure it was there at all.

He stood a few paces away and watched as the two entities—unmistakable now as the glowing golden forms of a woman and her daughter—emerged from the water. The light glowed brightest over those areas that might have been inappropriate for him to see, but in addition to that the woman had golden wings that she wrapped around her daughter as they emerged. Their hair flowed as if still submerged, though they were not. Their eyes were bright—not made from the light, but the light seemed to flow from within.

"Thank you," she said, looking at him. As she did, the light formed around her and her daughter, then subsided to leave behind golden armor that perfectly matched his.

He stared in confusion, then finally nodded.

"We thought you were one of them," she said and gestured to the rocks at the edge of the cavern. They walked together and sat, the daughter staring up at him with wide eyes.

"One of... whom?" he asked, finally finding his voice.

"Our enemy," she replied. "They look very much like you in their natural state, before you took off your headpiece, that is."

"My helmet?" He blinked, trying to comprehend this. "What about...the dragons?"

"Ah, you mean our other form." The woman smiled, and as she did he realized the glow had mostly faded to the extent that now she and her daughter were starting to look mostly human but with golden eyes and skin that seemed to sparkle in the light. "We are what you might call shape shifters. Judging by your expression, I assume you do not have another shape?"

He laughed at this. "No, as much as I sometimes wish. But have you come into contact with humans before? How is it that you speak my language?"

"We simply speak and our minds translate by receiving your brainwaves to ensure we understand each other."

The translation caused a momentary sharp pain in the back of his head, but he nodded, trying to understand. Nothing to date had set him or his companions up for anything like this. When they'd set out through the gate, they'd all discussed the idea of finding life on other planets, but Trent had always assumed they'd find a fish with legs or something like gremlins. But this?

"He's not dangerous, Mother?" the girl asked, looking between the two.

The mom shook her head, though her eyes met his. "Though your kind might be. Am I wrong?"

He thought about this, realizing that if she was able to somehow use his brainwaves to translate language, she could probably tell if he lied. "We *can* be, but if the others were ever to meet you, I would do everything possible to ensure they wouldn't be."

"You helped my daughter when she was trapped," she said. "I see a worthy warrior in you, one in need of healing." Gesturing to the pool of water, she added, "Please."

He blinked, looking between her and the water. "You want me to…what? Go in there?"

"Bathe in the healing waters. It is our gift to you."

"I…" He was going to argue that he didn't need a bath and that he didn't need healing, but neither was true. Still, the idea of going into waters that caused everything to glow sent his mind racing with ideas of nuclear waste and thoughts of chemical reactions.

"It's safe," she said. "You will stay with us for now, but first you must be washed of your impurities."

"Where I come from, we don't just bathe in unknown places."

"And yet, you aren't where you come from."

For a moment, he considered this, then nodded and stood. He walked over to the edge of the pool and then glanced back to see that they were both watching him. Clearing his throat, he glanced down at his armor, hoping he wouldn't have to spell it out for them.

The mom cocked her head and then smiled as if she were amused. She nodded, averted her gaze, and turned her daughter away.

Feeling for the release of his Space Corps armor, he realized how sore and in pain he really was. His ribs ached and pain shot up his side, leaving his arm numb. The chest-plate fell away with a crash, and then he commenced with removing the rest until he was wearing nothing but his boxers. All of the action since crash landing had gotten him quite worked up, but now he caught a whiff of himself and realized how badly he really did need a bath.

A deep breath pulled in the scent of water unlike anything he had ever known. It was as if one could smell rays of sun trickling through leaves on a warm spring day.

He glanced back and saw that they still had their gazes averted, so he removed the boxers, shivered in the cool breeze, and then stepped into the water. Only, it didn't feel like water. Instead, it was as if he had just stepped into a pool of warm mist, as if there were such a thing.

With each step he took, his surroundings grew warmer and the mist-water began to glow. Soon he had golden light up to his chest and he was turning in it, running his fingers through it. He watched as golden tendrils slipped over and around him.

A breath brought with it a sweet taste that reminded him of a fruit he'd tried once on a trip to Laos, but he couldn't quite put his finger on which one it had been. Light wafted up and into his mouth, sending tingling warmth through his body. The healing process had begun, except there was something else to it, like a strength he'd never known he had was now open and available to him for the first time.

He turned, looking down at his body, and smiled. This was the best he had ever felt. For the first time since landing, he didn't have the sense of anxiety hanging over him, the dread at being stranded on this planet.

All was peaceful.

When he turned and walked out of the pool, he emerged to find the woman standing there, waiting. How odd, he thought, that he wasn't self-conscious about his nudity. It simply didn't seem to matter anymore.

A glance down showed he needn't have been concerned because golden light shone over him as it had on them before. With a wave of her hand, the light brightened and then faded, leaving behind a layer of clothing and new body armor—gold like her own.

"What… is this?" he asked.

"I wasn't sure it would happen," she replied. "The planet has accepted you, granted you some of her strength."

Every muscle in him seemed to be alive, more like they were his friends who would give their all to accomplish whatever he set his mind to rather than simply part of his body. He moved his arm and observed that the armor was barely noticeable, as if he was still nude, but when he tapped his forearms together they clanged like metal.

Part of him felt completely at ease there, but a small voice in his head kept asking question after question. What had happened to him? Was this some sort of magic? Were all of the dragons—or whatever these people called themselves when in the form that resembled what he knew as dragons—shape shifters like these two?

Next they led him to a different part of the cave where golden, waving plants grew. They showed him how to eat these and to drink from the golden lake, and they began working with him on his ability to manipulate the powers around him.

As he lost track of time and space, he found himself whole, connected, one with the world and one with the universe. When he met his enemy again, he knew he'd be ready.

16

SHRINA: SHARED INTELLIGENCE GROUP, AMERICAN BRANCH

The team had barely had a chance to catch their breath and unwind when Richards stormed in, glanced around, and settled his gaze on Shrina.

"They want you," he said.

"What?"

"Just come. You'll see, or… hear."

She frowned, glancing around at Roy and the others' looks of confusion, but followed without another question.

"There we were, thinking we had to try and interrogate the bastard, when guess who walks in?" Richards paused for effect but didn't really expect an answer. "Secretary of State Veles, that's who. He tells us not to worry, that he has it under control. I'm wondering what the hell State has to do with any of this, but then he explained his past and his involvement in a new program that's related to mind manipulation. And… it's working."

They exited the passage into a room that looked through mirrors into an interrogation room where the captured vampire sat. Veles and two of his men were with him.

"Go ahead," Richards said into his comms.

Veles nodded, hit something on his wrist piece, and said, "Again, tell us why you're here."

The vampire stared blankly at him for a moment, the red nearly gone from his eyes, and said, "I… honestly don't remember. There was a name—Shrina Collins." Shrina felt her heart racing at that, but it only confirmed her suspicions at the building where she'd rescued Prestige. She kept listening. "I see images, like… I don't know."

"Try," Veles said, leaning forward. "Please try."

A look of pain went through the vampire, and he said, "There was a jet… we were overseas… and caves… darkness, and… and…"

"Spit it out."

"A dragon."

Veles laughed, looked through the mirror in Shrina's direction with a look of confusion, then said, "A dragon?"

"Not a real one. But in those caves, it felt like it

could be at times. No, a carving or a statue… with eyes like emeralds."

The others were starting to look doubtful, but Shrina stepped back, hand to her chest. If her heart kept beating like that, she was certain she'd pass out. Images of patterns and horse paintings and the dragon flashed through her mind from the moment before they'd pulled her out of her enhancements.

Her head started to spin and she stumbled out of there, looking for water and maybe somewhere to sit until the dizziness passed.

"Are you all right, Agent Collins?" Richards asked, but his voice faded out behind her as she entered the hallway and the door shut.

How was it possible this man—no, this vampire—was describing what she'd seen in that nightmare? Was it possible it was a coincidence? That didn't seem likely. And what was worse about the whole situation was that it seemed to tie together what they'd done to her and what these things were. Those so-called vampires might be failed experiments, something the government had tried and ended up making a huge mistake.

The bigger implication for her was that maybe they had messed up on her, too, and soon she would become one of these *vampires*. She had to keep her fingers crossed that that wouldn't happen, but it still didn't explain why they were after her.

"Collins," Richards said, now joining her. His normally stern face was creased with worry. "What happened in there?"

"A dizzy spell," she explained. "Nothing more."

"Well, if you'd stayed you would've seen that he's given us locations on a map where they might be. I know none of you have had a chance to rest, and you earned it back there, but… We're sending in the team."

"Roger that," she said. "You can count on us."

"Collins…"

"Yeah?"

"I knew Trent." His eyes showed compassion, and it was sweet that he thought that was what was bothering her, so she didn't interrupt. "He and I worked together for a bit. I was a corporal under him back when he was still a staff sergeant. You know who he used to talk about when he'd had one too many at the bar?"

She frowned. "Why?"

"I don't know. I'm not saying the guy was in love with you or anything. I don't know. But he certainly had you on his mind. You made an impression."

Shrina considered that, nodded, and said, "Thanks," before walking off to join the rest of the team. After a couple of paces, she paused and turned back to him. "Any word on when they'll send a team after them?"

"Veles thought you might ask," Richards said with a chuckle. "Seems you're friends with everyone, huh?"

What a thought. In reality, she had always put too much time and energy into her work. "So?"

"They're working on it, but they want to ensure it's safe and that there won't be any more attacks. Plus, there's worry that these things came through and that it's somehow related."

"I don't believe that for a second," she replied. "And I'm going to prove it."

"Do that," he said. "The quicker we unravel this whole mess, the quicker that rescue party goes up there."

Talk about pressure. With a sigh and a thought about Trent, wondering how this image of the dragon tied into it all, she returned to the others.

"Let me guess," Roy said as she entered. He was leaning against the wall as if he'd been waiting for her. "We're going to have to postpone that drink, huh?"

She nodded.

"Figures. Vampire cock-blockers."

"Excuse me?" She wasn't exactly in the mood for jokes, and the implication annoyed her.

"Ignore me," he said, frowning, and pushed off from the wall before heading off to sit with the SEALs.

She shook her head, mad at herself. For so long she'd been struggling to be part of something like this, to make a difference. The idea of living a normal life, of normal relationships and friendships, felt so alien.

Instead of dwelling on it, she began to gear up. She checked her rifle and HUD on her helmet's faceplate, making sure everything was working. The best route would be to finish this and then figure out her life. One step at a time.

An idea struck her. As crazy as it was, she charged back out through the main door, fully suited up, and headed back toward the interrogation room. When she saw Veles in the hall, she called out to him. The two men at his side turned, hands on their pistols, but he waved them down.

"Good to see you again, Shrina," he said. "Sorry it's not under better circumstances."

"I want to go."

"Isn't that what you all are getting ready to d—"

"No, sir. Secretary Veles, I want to go up there with the rescue mission." She took a deep breath. "I'll talk it over with Richards or whoever I need to. But when you send a team up in space to find out what happened, I want in."

He looked impressed but unsure. With his politician's smile, he patted her on her armored shoulder and said, "I'll see what I can do."

"Sir," she said, "I want better than that. If I can get clearance on my side, see that it's done. Please."

He started to turn, but hesitated, then nodded. "I would say there are tests, issues with space travel and danger, but you've had the enhancements already and seem to be doing fine. Prove yourself on this next mission—eliminate the threat—and I can't see any reason why they wouldn't want you."

"That's a yes?" she asked, determined to have a concrete answer.

He laughed. "Yes, Shrina. Yes."

With that she gave him a smile, moved as if to hug him, but then pulled back and said, "Thank you," before jogging back to the main room, her armored boots clanging down the hallway.

Now she had a real objective, not just a mission. A goal. And once she set her mind to achieving a goal, she always made it happen.

17

ESPINOZA: SPACE, UNKNOWN PLANET A

Heading back out into the same territory he almost died in the night before—and also had one of the most memorable experiences of his life in—was a nerve-racking experience. That was to say nothing of the fact that now Gunnery Sergeant Ellins was leading the group, a woman who had kissed him passionately when they all thought they'd die as the ship was crashing onto the planet. His palms were sweaty just thinking about it, though he kind of liked the distraction from other thoughts that threatened to overwhelm him, thoughts like the fact that they could walk into a vampire ambush at any minute and that they had no idea what else was waiting for them out there.

They found the cave, stopping for lunch and a break to get a sense of direction. With Franco on watch, Ellins waved Espinoza and Kim in close, drawing a map in the soft dirt with the butt of her rifle.

"We're here, relative to the ship," she said, indicating a circle she drew and then a line to several ovals that could be hills. "Which direction do you think it was that the altercation took place?"

Espinoza's mind filled with images of Kim's flesh, her eyes as she moaned, and he fought hard not to say it was here, in this cave.

Kim, however, apparently had a clearer mind because she indicated a spot on the makeshift map. "The tree we marked was here."

"Ah, yes," Espinoza said, clearing his mind. He indicated a spot to the right of there. "Since they attacked from this direction, I'd assume we can head that way and maybe find something."

Ellins glanced at him, curious. "You seem distracted. Head in the game?"

"I'm good, Gunny."

"Right. Be sure you are."

She pulled out her rations—a fancy MRE that, surprisingly or not, hadn't seemed to change in the last couple of hundred years. They were still chicken and rice with a pound cake, or maybe Skittles if one was lucky. Espinoza had meatloaf, which always felt like a delicacy to him since nobody really ate the stuff anymore other than in MREs.

"Where were you two from, before all this?" Ellins asked.

Since he had a full mouth, Kim spoke up. "The Koreas, actually. Northern part, though my parents immigrated when I was young. Part of why I joined up, I guess, to feel real American. Now, I'm real Earther, I guess." She chuckled. "Never would've thought they'd pick me to go into space."

"Why not?"

"Aside from being born overseas, I lived in Cali my whole life and never left. Even boot camp and my first duty station were in the San Diego area. So I finally get out to see the world and it's from space. Go figure."

Ellins laughed. "Can't say I relate. I was one of those who got around." She shot Espinoza a glance at that—one he wasn't sure how to read—but then continued. "I was part of the attack on New Origins out in Dubai. Man, I wish I could've been up on Space Station Horus to see their CEO fall, you know what I mean? Pricks, all of them."

"You were in Dubai?" Espinoza asked, impressed. "Everyone talks about that mission. It's legendary."

"Yeah, well, most of it went down on the space

station. We basically arrived and they surrendered, minus a little scuffle."

"Still, that's badass." He beamed, then realized he was staring and looked away.

"And you, Espi?" Kim said with a knowing grin. "Did you get around much?"

"Moving around, seeing the world?" he said and shrugged. "Honestly, I'm from Ohio. Never had much reason to travel growing up."

"Ohio?"

"What? You thought I'd say Tijuana or something? That I'd always stared across the border, wishing I could be an American, so here I am?" He laughed when her expression showed she kind of *had* thought it would be something like that. "Nah, straight up Ohio, all the way. Thing is, I got involved with all these kids who wanted to be great writers, obsessed with the Ohio writing seminars, and I kinda rebelled against that at one point. We're living in a world where corporations try to make moves against the government, and we're on the cusp of space exploration with a gateway to the stars. How was I going to justify sitting around all day arguing the finer points of poetry by such greats as Elgis Falcon?"

"Damn," Ellins said, impressed. "Most reading I

ever did was stories about Ancient Greek warriors and whatnot. Maybe the military heart of mine."

"Jamie Hawke fan here," Kim said guiltily.

"Agh, say it isn't so," Ellins replied with a cough.

"I actually haven't heard of her. Him?" Espinoza admitted.

"Total porn disguised as science fiction and whatnot," Ellins explained. "Picked one up once and it was a major turn on, but that's why I had to stop. I was like, why not just go meet a guy and have fun instead of reading about it?"

"A girl can do both," Kim countered with a laugh.

"And this is my cue to relieve Franco," Ellins said, tucking away the half-eaten MRE for later. "Finish up and give him a few minutes to eat, then we're on our way."

Espinoza realized he'd been forgetting to eat, so he quickly stuffed a few bites in his face, watching Kim as she flicked Skittles into her mouth.

"Word porn, huh?" he asked with a full mouth.

She shrugged. "Everyone has their thing. Funny part is, that stuff's all written for guys. But I don't know, I like getting into your minds, seeing what you like. As twisted as you all like to think you are, trust me, women are more so."

"No arguments here," he said.

"So, did it happen?" Franco said, entering the

conversation with a grin. "I missed the three-way, didn't I?"

"Get your head out of the gutter," Kim said with a wink to Espinoza, as if their conversation hadn't just been in similar places.

He shrugged and dug in. "Just let me kill some vampires, and I'm good. Think it's like those old shows? Stakes through the heart and whatnot?"

"Don't mention steaks," Kim said, rolling her eyes. "God, I'd kill for a steak right now, through the heart, sure, but preferably in my mouth."

"Um…" Espinoza pursed his lips, trying to think of a way to tell her that was a lame connection.

"Shut up, poet," she said when she saw he wasn't coming up with anything to say. "What was your last meal, Franco?"

"It wasn't a death sentence," Franco said, meaning it like a joke but instantly frowning at his own words. "Huh, maybe it was. Damn, now I regret having opted for a bowl of Cocoa Puffs as my last meal on Earth."

"Nothing wrong with that," Espinoza said. "I had a salad with turkey, the lunchmeat kind, torn up on my ghetto salad without any dressing."

"That's horrible," Kim said, scrunching her nose.

"What was yours?" Espinoza asked.

"I skipped it," she said, smiling proudly. "That

way, I'd have something to look forward to when I got home."

"Which means… your lunch was your last meal," Franco argued, stuffing more food into his mouth.

Kim's expression soured. "Damn. That's not—no, that doesn't count."

"Why, what'd you have for lunch?"

"Dino chicken nuggets," she mumbled.

Espinoza and Franco shared a look and then a laugh.

"Tell me you have kids," Franco said.

"Or nephews and nieces," Espinoza threw in, not wanting to think that the woman he'd slept with last night already had kids. Not that there'd be anything wrong with that, but the idea scared him.

She shook her head. "You have your Cocoa Puffs, and I have my dino chicken nuggets. Deal with it."

"Hey, I still make pancakes shaped like Mickey Mouse," Espinoza admitted. "Once a month, I just eat whatever the hell I want and usually I opt for a breakfast of Mickey Mouse pancakes with some cheesecake for dessert. The kind with strawberries on it."

"Okay, this conversation is making me hungry and depressed," Kim said, staring down at her finished MRE. "I know I'm full, but my mouth is watering."

"Hit the road?" Franco said, scarfing down the last of his main meal and saving the other packets for later.

Espinoza and Kim agreed, so they all went out to join the gunny and start the trek to find the marked tree. Since they were entering possibly dangerous territory, the gunny had them keep comms open and stay alert.

"Anything moves out here, assume it's an enemy," Ellins said.

"Roger that," Franco replied. The other two kept on, silent. It wasn't a time for jokes.

Espinoza's HUD wasn't picking up anything out of the ordinary, but he wasn't sure he completely trusted it out there. Before long they came to a series of trees, some blown over, but one that looked like maybe, just maybe, it could have been the one with the marking. It was their best bet, so they turned in the direction he and Kim were fairly positive they'd seen the vampires attack from and carried on.

For some time they marched, watching the shadows move across the red dirt and nearby hills, cautious of what might be waiting with each step.

"Not exactly your preschool sandbox," Ellins said with a sigh.

"Gunny?" Kim asked.

"Just... sorry. My nephew, I was picking him up

and dropping him off at school every day, and they had these red wood chips around the sand box. This all reminds me of him and that school, but..."

There was a long silence.

"I didn't know you had a nephew," Espinoza said.

Ellins grunted. "Started to think about the little guy like a son, what with his mom out of the picture. She abandoned them, something to do with drugs. Stupid bitch."

"Damn." Espinoza had his cousins who'd been through something similar with their parents, so he'd seen close up how painful that could be.

"Sorry, you all don't need to hear this," Ellins said, her voice close to cracking. "Not from your gunny."

"We might be all the family and friends any of us have left," Kim said. "I know that's the worst thing to say right now. I should say not to worry, that we'll all be back soon, I guess, but we all know that's a pile of horse manure. So as far as I'm concerned, speak up, Gunny."

Ellins laughed. "The gentle touch of a female Marine."

"Hey, I do what I can."

"It's tough on all of us," Espinoza chimed in, not sure what to say and feeling like an idiot for speaking up at all. "My mom nearly killed me herself when she found out I was joining the Corps. I can't imagine she'd be so happy right now if she had any idea what I was up to."

"She doesn't know where you are?" Ellins asked with surprise.

"She's… sick. Being taken care of but doesn't quite remember one day to the next anymore. I figured adding stress and anxiety to the equation wouldn't help much." A sorrow gripped him and he felt the next step harder to make but pushed through. For the first time, he realized his last visit with his mom might really be his last.

"You'll see her again," Ellins said, as if reading his thoughts. "Just like I'm going to see my nephew again. Count on that."

"I'll hold you to it," he replied. If he was going to be stuck on this planet, confused about a weird love triangle of sorts, he was glad it was with these two.

"All y'all are gonna make me cry," Franco said, then scoffed. "Can we shut the hell up and just kill us some aliens or whatever?"

They laughed, but moved on in silence.

Kim was the first to spot the ship, turning and motioning the others down, then pointing to her right. They all hit the deck, then got into a good viewing position. Sure enough, half-buried out there at the edge of one of the sloping hills was one of their ships. It was out of commission, judging by half a wing missing, but from where they were there was no sign of the comms equipment being damaged.

"My screen's not showing any sign of survivors," Ellins said. "You all picking up anything?"

"Negative," Kim replied. The other two weren't either.

"We'll check the vicinity, then set up two guards while the other two ensure it's safe within."

They followed her lead, descending the hill and moving along the hillside to the right first, then breaking and darting across to the other hillside where the ship was located. Still no signs of life.

"No way they abandoned it," Espinoza said as the team drew closer.

"Unless they're locals," Kim said. "I'm still not convinced these things are people."

"What?" Franco said, baffled.

"You saw them. Red, glowing eyes, those teeth. Considering they arrived soon after we opened the gateway to the stars… do the math."

"I'm sure you're not alone in that thought," Ellins said. "But none of us really knows, do we?"

Kim shrugged. "Not saying I know, Gunny. But I'm not going to feel bad about shooting one of their heads off, thinking they might be human or something. Hell no."

"Damn right," Franco said, scanning the tops of

nearby hills. "One of those things comes near me—BAM! Right between the eyes."

"Good. You and me," Ellins said, gesturing to Franco, "we're going on that way to make sure it's secure. Then, you loop back up to the hill to watch for incoming hostiles. Kim and Espinoza, you two know the most about comms equipment. Check it out, but don't forget to clear the ship."

Espinoza nodded and they got to it. He and Kim ran for the ship, and it was hard not to marvel at the speed and grace with which she moved in her suit. They'd had their enhancements for a few months now, training and learning how to best take advantage of the terrain and their opponents, but it still felt surreal.

At the rear of the ship, she stopped, rifle held up, and waited for him.

"Do it to it," he said, and she nodded, moving to the partially open rear ramp. He followed her, having to jump to reach it since it was end up. When they were in, they had to hold onto the sides to keep from sliding. They kept their rifles ready in the other hand. At the base of the cargo hold, they were able to move along what had been a wall but was now twisted to almost form a floor.

"Clear," Espinoza said, checking the corners and then back the way they'd come.

"Clear," Kim echoed, moving along and checking the next room.

From there, they made it to the bridge and cleared it. Then Espinoza went back to the door and shoved it open, checking for incoming as he gave the gunny an update.

"All clear in here," he said. "Kim's looking into the comms, but it looked fine at a glance."

"I'm here, Gunny," Kim said over the comms. "Trying to start up now and see if there's any way to send something back through to Earth."

"Make it quick," Franco's voice chimed in. "I have movement."

"How many?" Ellins asked.

"Unclear. For now, all I can see is dust. They're moving fast." A pause, then, "Shit, shit, we need to get out of here."

"What is it, Corporal?" Ellins shouted.

"Give me two seconds," Kim broke in, interrupted by Franco's heavy breathing.

"It's not them. It's something else." Espinoza said. "Something's moving through the earth. Something large."

"You heard him. Get out of there," Ellins said. "Let's go!"

"Just a... Dammit!" Kim moved back to Espinoza's side, shaking her head as she said into the comms, "It's not good. Power's up here, but it looks like part of the equipment was damaged. I'm going to see if I can find out what."

"Not if you want to live," Franco said, and Espinoza frowned, exiting to look up and see Franco bounding down the hillside, a cloud of dust visible behind him.

Then there was something else, too—several forms moving as if in pursuit, but they weren't firing. No, they weren't chasing Franco. They were fleeing from whatever it was back there.

"Come on, Kim," Espinoza said, turning back and looking to find her on the side of the ship, investigating it. "NOW!"

She glanced up and cursed, then said, "Hold them off."

"It's not them we're worried about," he said, and just then, around the corner of the hill, the moving dirt appeared. It was massive, the size of a long tunnel that was wide enough for at least four cars, and it was charging right at them.

"Holy…" She didn't even finish the sentence but took off running with Espinoza at her side. They were joined by Ellins off to their right, and Franco brought up the rear. He was looking behind him and shooting wildly at the other forms, possibly the vampires that had attacked Espinoza.

"Cease fire," Ellins shouted. "Just focus on getting your ass out of here!"

He did as ordered, starting to close the distance between them. The vampires weren't firing either, just running as the monstrous creature beneath the ground slammed into the ship. Espinoza and the others spun to see, watching with shock as a layer of dirt broke free and knocked the ship sideways. Whatever it was, the beast had scales the color of rust and sand, and moved like a sandworm. It circled, cutting the vampires off from the ship, and then slammed it again.

Apparently done, it circled one more time, then sunk back into the ground as if none of it had happened.

"The signal," Kim said with a gasp. "The comms signal was working, though it wasn't getting out to Earth. Still, it could've attracted that thing."

"We can figure all that out later," Ellins said, bringing her rifle up to fire. "We've got company."

She was right. With the immediate threat over, the vampires were charging at them.

The first shot rang out, grazing one of the vampire's legs and causing it to stumble. A loud rumbling started up again, and then the earth rose as the sandworm came right for Espinoza and his group.

Before Ellins could fire another shot, Espinoza reached out and put his hand on her forearm.

She looked at him, then back to the approaching sandworm. They all seemed to realize that the shot had likely attracted it, but Franco was the first to act on it. He had a grenade in his hand, which he lobbed away to their left, and said, "Go!" pointing the other way.

They all ran, and a glance back showed that the vampires were now blocked from view by the approaching sandworm.

KA-BOOM! The grenade sounded. For a few heart-stopping beats, the sandworm kept coming but then started circling around, moving back toward the sound of the explosion.

Espinoza was quite glad to see that nobody else was stopping to see what happened next. He only wanted to get the hell out of there and never have to deal with another of those monstrosities again. They ran and ran, and then they ran some more.

When they reached the cave, they threw themselves in, tearing off helmets and reaching for their water. All of them were close to hyperventilating.

"At least," Ellins said, "it wasn't a total waste of time."

"How's that?" Franco spat back.

"We know where the ship is and some of the vampires."

"And we know what local threat we're up against," Espinoza chimed in, "though I'd argue that ignorance is bliss in this case."

"Yeah, we know how we're going to die," Franco said, glaring. "Wonderful."

"Not necessarily," Kim countered.

"To which part?" Ellins asked.

"Dying. I think we can get off this planet, or at least get a message back to Earth, anyway. The rest is up to them, I guess."

"Explain."

"The comms system on their ship isn't fried. It's just not connecting. I think it needs a part replacement—a part our ship happens to have."

Everyone stared at her, Espinoza feeling a sense of hope he'd been starting to wonder if he'd ever feel again.

"Well then," Ellins said, "we have our mission. Impossible? Maybe. But hell, what're Marines for if not accomplishing the impossible?"

18

SHRINA: TUNISIA

"We're setting down at the edge of Tunis, then making our way from there," Richards said as their jet passed over the waters north of Algeria. They had just finished their meals and were ready to go. "The idea is to head down from there, not let them know we're coming, if possible, and strike hard and fast."

Shrina frowned at the way Roy glanced over at her. He looked away before their eyes could meet. When she looked away, she could tell he was looking at her again. The difficulty in that was figuring out if he was looking because they were going into danger or if it was because the words 'hard and fast' had just been used. She'd been around macho men long enough to know that word choices of that sort led to wandering minds.

"Local intel says our destination is out where they used to film some old Starry Wars movies or something—"

"Star Wars," Roy corrected him, suddenly sitting very alert.

"Well, we have a history buff among us," Chung chimed in, laughing. "Look at that."

"Just… any chance they have the old movie sets still up?"

"Doubt it," Richards said. "After this many years, that sort of stuff falls apart. Can we focus now?"

"Right. But to be clear—Star Wars."

"Yes, got it." Richards said and then hesitated, laughed, and continued. "We don't want any mistakes here. Humanity can't afford them. That means we need at least one alive, and we need to ensure none escape to tell the others we're coming. Got that?"

"We think there are others, then?" Chung asked.

"Have you been paying attention? They're everywhere. In fact…" He pulled up his wrist computer and swiped so an image appeared on the ceiling of the jet. It was a headline of an attack on government offices in Tokyo. "Here's what you all missed while you were training."

Shrina watched the footage in horror, her mind

going back to her little sister. She was safe—she had to be.

"New sources point to there being multiple groups, not just one concerted effort," Richards went on to explain. "We might not be fighting a central force, which means we have to learn more about them—where this started and what makes them tick. Mostly, the attacks seem to be focused on trying to take control, or in the case of the launch… well, we're not sure yet. As odd as it is, the best guess is to get to space."

"And then there were the other seemingly random attacks," Roy pointed out.

The others started speculating about those, throwing out words like terrorism and random acts of vampire violence. It seemed that only Shrina was aware anyone had been after her specifically, and she didn't mean to see that information shared until she understood why.

Everyone stopped talking when the captain's voice came on, saying, "Prepare for landing."

The jet came in fast, not providing much time to look out over Tunisia, but Shrina was too busy thinking anyway. At least her enhancements had helped with motion sickness because the jet wasn't coming in smoothly. She leaned back, closed her eyes, and tried not to think about the horrible guilt over leaving her family behind. It wasn't like she'd had a choice, but not being with them sucked. Then there was Alicia—for all she knew, her sister could be out there, dead on some street or homeless. Not being able to do a damn thing about it ate at Shrina's soul.

Oddly, flying into this country didn't take her back to the last time they'd been there together, though. Instead, she was reminded of setting up forts as children. As the older sister, Alicia hadn't always made time for playing with Shrina, but when she did, it was the best feeling in the world. There'd been one time when they'd dragged out all of the chairs and torn down the curtains to make their fort, setting it up with cushions and pretending it was a grand Middle-Eastern court with Alicia as the queen. Just a silly game, but when Alicia had tried to run after Shrina for stealing the crown, the fort had all fallen down and a snow globe they'd been using as a weight for the sheets landed on Shrina's toe. Alicia ran off and returned with ice, then held her, stroking her head as their mom had always done until the tears stopped.

It was moments like those that Shrina knew were, of course, long gone, but she really missed them. Even though it was all part of growing up, she at least wanted to be able to sit with her sister and laugh about stupid life mistakes, share a piece of carrot cake for a birthday, or have them over to meet the family, if that ever happened.

In another life, perhaps.

Before long they were setting down and then off the jet, moving out along the edges of the city to their transportation. The agreement was that they wouldn't be seen coming from the airport in case the enemy had eyes on the situation.

Shrina had only been to this part of the world once before and that was when she'd secretly met up with Alicia and Marick before the two had gone into hiding. It wasn't the same, at all. Even though it had been built up the last time she'd been there, it was nothing like the tall metal buildings with their arched bridges, domed roofs, and brightly lit multi-colored glass art that now filled Tunis. In fact, it was nothing like what she'd first expected when looking up pictures of the place. Once upon a time, the city had consisted of old buildings of brick and stone, crumbling ruins surrounded by sand-covered streets and muddy rivers. Oh, how the world had changed.

On the outskirts of town, they met up with a contact who had all the details previously arranged. The old man smiled, showed them the way, and then departed without a word.

"What exactly do you suppose he thinks we're up

to here?" Chung asked with a smirk, watching the old man go. "A bunch of Americans show up with equipment like this and they point us to jeeps and send us off into the desert. Some kind of battle royale, maybe?"

Landon laughed. "I'm sure there're plenty of dickwads out there they're hoping we'll take out."

"If they knew the truth, they'd piss themselves," Chung replied.

"Unfortunately, none of us do," Shrina chimed in.

"We know these vampires are camped in their backyard, and it's up to us to kill 'em."

Shrina noted the challenging look in Chung's eyes, so she just nodded and said, "And we will."

The teams split up into three jeeps—Shrina with Chung, Roy, and Landon—and the journey began. By the time they'd left the main roads behind and found themselves largely surrounded by smaller villages, rolling hills, and palm-tree-scattered deserts, the sun was low in the sky.

Shrina stared out from the driver-side rear seat, wondering what they'd find out there. She closed her eyes, imagining herself in the heat of the moment, running out with guns blazing and leaping over enemy corpses. It was all still so surreal, but she knew she was as ready as she was going to be.

"There was this time in the War," Landon started

to say, glancing back at Roy via the rearview mirror. Landon was driving, Chung was in the passenger seat, and Roy was beside Shrina in the back. "I swear to the gods I thought I was gonna die. There we were, our mechs charging in, and all of a sudden enemy jets are flying overhead, dropping all kinds of shit on us."

"You were at the battle of Kelong?" Chung asked, impressed.

"Damn right, I was." He met Shrina's gaze for a moment, a fact that Chung noticed with irritation. "Thing is, you can survive for a long time in those mechs. I took out two of those jets before they got to me with napalm and explosions that rocked the ground, and soon I was literally in the ground, being buried. I'm freaking out, right? I mean, buried alive. For all I know, I'm never coming out of there. And then it's all piling on, more and more, and the damn mech can't move. I'm freaking out, right?"

"What'd you do?" Roy asked.

"Panicked, pissed myself—gave up. And then realized I could break through the hatch and simply walk out of there. Even though the mech was buried and worthless, I could still fit through the openings between the rocks. I walked up there to see that all the jets had been taken out by surgical strikes. There was fire and chaos all around me, but the fighting had stopped. Ended up hitching a ride on a mech that belonged to this one hottie, and then I rode—er," he said and glanced at Shrina, then away. "I mean, yeah, I got out of there."

"The point?" Shrina asked, ignoring Roy's grin.

"Sometimes when you think you're down and out, you just gotta look at the situation from a different point of view. Think outside the box, or in my case, the mech."

"Gods… I can't imagine," Shrina said. Being buried alive was definitely not on the top of her bucket list.

"Gods?" Chung asked. "Tell me you're not… not into the old ways?"

"Me?" Shrina asked. "Oh, no. Just a saying."

Landon chuckled. "Me, I don't believe in shit. Well, I believe in shit, but no religion, and in my mind they're the same thing."

"That's confusing," Roy said.

"You got a different view on it all?" Landon asked.

"Titanian, through and through," Roy said, straight faced.

After a moment of silence, the other two started laughing.

"No way," Landon said. "No way in hell are you a Titanian."

Roy shrugged.

"You're saying you're going up to Titan someday, and you believe there'll be a war between some risen Titan from—wait for it—Titan because some scientist named it that years ago."

"To be fair, they found ruins on Mars, and we still don't know where those came from or what they're all about," Shrina said. "Not to mention the gateway itself. For all we know, there could be a Titan or some strange being that resembles one, and maybe it will fight some form of gods on Earth." She lit up, leaning forward. "Maybe the vampires are the so-called gods!"

"Or we are," Roy said, shrugging. "Prophesies often have some truth to them, and you saw the way Richards healed after cutting himself. You did that back in the day, people would think you're a god. But… no, I don't really follow the beliefs."

"No?" Shrina was a little let down. She'd heard of these people before but hadn't encountered many of them.

"But I was raised Titanian," he said, noticing her expression. "My parents went up to Horus even before the fall of New Origins to study under priestess Yerbuna. I stayed behind to finish up school and serve." He turned to Shrina. "What's your story?"

"Pssh, you don't know?" Landon said. "Our girl here's a presidential favorite. Helped with the siege in Dubai."

"Get out of here," Chung said, glaring at Shrina even fiercer than she had before. This woman did not like competition.

"Yeah, her sister was even part of the biotech wars. Had a husband who was one of the original enhanced. O.E., baby."

"Had?" Roy asked.

"They both went missing after that," Shrina explained. "And thanks for telling everyone my life's story, Landon."

"Every one of them went missing," Landon went on, as if not even hearing her. "All the enhanced went into hiding, not wanting to be slaves of the governments."

"We know that part," Roy said.

"Oh, you were interested in Shrina having a sister if she's going to keep ignoring your requests for a date?" Landon said with a laugh. "Maybe she'll go out with me and I can tell you how it went."

"I'd sooner date Chung here before either of you, and that isn't happening," Shrina said and motioned to the way Chung was glaring at her. "Mostly because she's a bitch."

"Way to team build," Landon said with a chuckle.

Roy frowned, apparently not liking the way this conversation was going. "What about you, Chung? What's the deal?"

But Chung wasn't done glaring at Shrina, who was doing her best to pretend not to notice.

"Chung?"

"Oh, me?" Chung said and put on a smile real fast. "West Point, top of my class. They brought you boys for your muscle; they brought me for my brains."

Shrina couldn't help but notice how Chung had left her out of the equation.

They drove on, Chung talking about how she was actually quite good at sports, very athletic despite her size, and went on to tell an entire story about playing contact soccer with the big boys. Apparently, her shins could take more of a beating than any of them, as if that was the way to impress men.

"The best part, though, what I miss the most, was this place you could go to on Sunday mornings for brunch," Chung went on. "The best pumpkin pancakes in the world, I'm telling you. Oooh, I'd kill for some of those pancakes when we kill these vampires."

"Deal," Landon said. "When this is over, I'm taking you out for pumpkin pancakes."

"Yeah?"

"Sure, the whole team. My treat. If that's what motivates you, it's my promise."

Judging by the expression on Chung's face, taking just her would've been more of an incentive, but she still smiled and said she'd love it.

"Pickles for me," Roy said.

"What?" Landon glanced over, confused.

"I'm a simple man," Roy replied. "For some reason, I've been craving pickles since we took off."

"I hear they have pomegranate trees around here," Shrina said. "Not anywhere close to pickles, but still… cool."

Roy laughed. "Sure, let's stop by on the way to kill the vampires and pick some pomegranates. Oh, and then we'd have red juice running down our chins and we could go deep undercover to learn all the vampire secrets."

They all laughed at that, but it was cut off by their comms buzzing.

"We've got incoming," Richards said over the comms, and Shrina frowned, leaning to get a look out the window. They were surrounded by desert now, the far-off image of Tunis almost like a mirage behind them. The sky to their right turned bright orange, and then the glint showed, followed by clouds of dust on the horizon.

"Moving east," Landon said. "Let's give 'em hell."

"One broke off, heading south. Cut 'em off!"

Landon veered left, putting himself and the jeep in the line of the enemy vehicle. Meanwhile, Roy was muttering about how pissed off he was that he wasn't going to see the old movie sets, or at least where they'd once been.

"What's up with you and that movie, anyway?" Landon asked.

"Movies," Roy replied. "Dammit, those films should be required viewing for everyone. Especially nowadays, with us going into space and all that."

"Right, because they got it right?"

"We *are* fighting some sort of vampire-like things," Chung pointed out. "Not much I'd doubt lately."

"True," Shrina said, glancing over to see if her agreement had earned any favor. Nope. Chung simply looked away. Whatever, they were there to fight vampires, not pout about a lack of attention.

"SHIT!" Landon shouted, swerving as a rocket went right past the jeep and exploded behind them.

The enemy jeep was in view now. A figure was on top, lowering a rocket launcher while another handed up a machine gun.

"Time to return fire," Roy said, rolling down the window and leaning out with his DD4 assault rifle. The first round of shots hit, but as soon as their bullets started pelting nearby sand, another round of shots came from Chung and the enemy bullets went wide as the shooter fell back and off the jeep.

Landon spun their jeep around, motioned for all of them to get out, and then followed with the grenade launcher. Thwoomp. Thwoomp. Ka-BOOM!

The front of the enemy jeep exploded, and a second later the other explosion hit so that it rocketed forward. Upon impact, it flipped, crushing whoever was sticking out of the top. Shrina was propped up against the side of the jeep away from their enemies, rifle at the ready. At the first sign of movement, she let the bullets fly, watching as blood splattered and aiming again.

"Don't let up!" she shouted. "Remember, they can heal too!"

The shooting continued, but one of the vampires made it from the enemy jeep, charging for them. As annoying as he could be, Landon proved that didn't affect his ability to fight. He jumped up onto the hood of the jeep, pulled out his Ka-Bar knife, and leaped to meet the enemy. They scuffled while the rest of the team kept firing at the other survivors, but then the vampire was up and running over the closest dune, blood seeping down its body from multiple stab wounds.

Shrina turned to pursue because Landon started taking fire from the survivors and had to get to cover. She charged, hitting the vampire with two good shots to the legs, but it still kept going. It disappeared over the dune and she jumped to the top. The sand gave way beneath her as she ran, which slowed her down, but she finally made it.

The vampire turned to her with crazed, bloodied eyes and smiled.

"Something funny?" she asked, aiming.

Another vampire slammed into her from behind, claws tearing at her armor, but it didn't penetrate and she was able to kick it off of her. Where the hell had he come from? She recovered and glanced around for her rifle, but then two more vampires rose up from the sand and converged on her. They had blades and one tried to fire a plasma rifle at her, but her armor's shield protected her.

The first vampire had her now, another clinging to her legs, and they took her down. She tried to struggle, turning desperately back to the dune and the sound of continued gunshots, hoping for help, but none came.

She let out a shout of agony, calling for backup through her comms, but they had her now, turned over and kneeling. She shut up—not because they forced her to but out of curiosity. In front of her was a vampire that seemed out of place from the others. He was tall and slender, almost willowy. His head was clean shaven, his eyes a deeper red and less glowing but firmer. Staring into his face, she was certain she recognized him from somewhere but couldn't place it.

"You?" he said, stepping forward. "I recognize you." Pulling up his wrist computer, he made a screen appear and started scrolling through it as he analyzed her.

She frowned as she eyed him, noting that the exoskeleton, New Origins uniform, and equipment weren't so different from her own. The way he spoke, in spite of his red eyes, made him appear just like any other enhanced human. But most shocking of all had to be the picture of herself now on his screen. It appeared to have been taken from surveillance footage and seemed to be of her meeting with Alicia and Marick.

When he held it up to her and scanned, the screen beeped and her outline went green before he stowed it.

"Take her," he said, turning around and motioning to the dune where two stealth pods rose up out of the sand. Each had a desert camo pattern, and she now saw that the jeeps had been a distraction.

She wasn't going anywhere with this son of a bitch. As they shoved her forward, she went with it —hard, like she was lunging—and they pulled back. She used that leverage to go back, swinging them forward and into each other, then kept up with the momentum and stomped through one of their knees,

"Set!" a third called out just as Shrina drew her pistol out and got a shot off.

The warning had been enough for Set to dodge, and he was on her before she could get off another shot. His eyes flared red and his claws jutted out, but he hesitated. With a curse, he threw her to the sand and kicked her once in the ribs with a force that felt like the heavens had fallen to crush her.

Along with the crack she heard, all sense of presence evaporated at once, and pain spread like rapid explosions across her insides and then out. She was gone—back home to a time when none of this had mattered. They were putting Alicia in her wedding dress and Shrina held her bouquet of roses while they dressed the bride in their grandmother's jewelry. Shrina had been so happy that day—happy for Alicia, but also happy because she'd seen the whole charade and realized it wasn't what she wanted anytime soon. Her life was about making a difference first, and while she knew those two things didn't have to be separate, the realization had been a relief, taking away the stress of it all. Then followed the dancing, partying, and watching the sunrise with the waterfall so close. It had been bliss, a day she wouldn't have minded reliving, watching that joy on her sister's face. Then it had all gone wrong when Alicia's husband went to space and Alicia was told that he was dead. She'd gone after them for the truth because she wouldn't accept it.

And somehow it had all led to this. She was sure of it. Maybe not her sister's involvement, but somehow she was certain it was all connected.

The memories faded as her consciousness returned and the pain took hold again. But this time she loved the pain because it told her she was still alive. Hands were on her, lifting her into a nearby pod.

She refused to let them take her, pain be damned. Thrashing about, she caught hold of one of their arms and was able to twist it in the way they'd shown her at the academy. The vampire yelped and nearly dropped her, but the other slammed her in the head with his elbow. More shooting pains, but what was a little bruise compared to what she'd already suffered?

A well-aimed kick caught him in the jaw and then both dropped her. Good timing, too, because just then Chung came leaping over the hill, bullets flying. A second later Roy was there, kneeling and putting bullets between eyes. Shrina rolled out of the way, trying to keep a low profile out of the line of fire, and then she saw something flying by overhead. It hit the ground and Set was out of there a second later. By the time Shrina was able to process why, it was almost too late except that Roy had her, thrusting two metal stakes into the ground. A blue energy shield went up just before the smart grenade went off. It exploded out first, with heat-seeking smaller explosives tearing through the remaining vampires moments later. More followed and targeted the stealth pods, knocking them down and setting them aflame.

Shrina's eyes roamed the bodies, looking for Set. Instead, she saw only footsteps. She'd never seen anything move as fast as he must've been moving to get out of there in time. She stumbled after him in pursuit, and Roy came to her aid. They crested the dune in time to see the flash of a blue light, and a form that looked like Set vanished. And that was it. He was gone, leaving only footprints behind.

"How the...?" Roy asked, but Shrina knew what had happened. She'd seen this sort of tech before on a man named Pete. Pete had borrowed it from Shrina's brother-in-law, who had obtained it in secret while on Space Station Horus. It was some sort of alien tech that worked to teleport, create shields, and more.

And the vampires had it.

It was confirmed in her mind then, no doubt about it. The vampires definitely had an alien connection. Whether they were simply humanoids or humans who'd been infected with something alien, she didn't know. All of the remaining vampires surrounding her were dead, but she had to hope the rest of her team had captured one of theirs because now more than ever she wanted answers.

"What did we just see?" Roy asked.

She turned to him and considered but then figured she might as well tell him on the way back to the others. They jogged back over the dune, weapons at the ready and curious at the silence. No more gunshots could mean victory or defeat. Before they were able to see the outcome, she'd told him the simple version of what she'd seen with Pete and why he'd had the suit with alien tech.

"How do we fight that?" Roy asked.

"Only the main one seemed to be equipped with it," she said. "My guess is they don't have many, if even more than that one. But what they're doing here? That's what I'd like to know."

"Recruiting," Landon said, appearing from their left.

The sight of him startled Shrina and she nearly went into attack mode, her mind taking a few seconds to process the sound of his voice and the sight of him. It didn't help that the orange glow of sunset was now glistening on the sand, creating deep shadows.

"We got 'em," Landon said, gesturing to the other jeeps and corpses. "No escapees."

Just as Shrina was about to correct him, Richards' jeep pulled up, sand clouds billowing behind it. He stepped out with a hand to his ear.

"Roger that, sir," he said, then turned to them and sighed, motioning for them to come closer. When they had, he looked at them, concerned. "This wasn't the only force. More of them seem to have evaded us, and satellites lost them in the city."

"What the hell," Chung said, eyes searching the sky as if she'd be able to see them. "This is bull."

"But not hopeless," Richards said, motioning to the jeep behind him. Three men emerged with a vampire clasped between them. He didn't have a bright glow, but it was there.

"There was another," Roy said, and then Shrina offered up the details. When they were done filling everyone in, Richards looked more worried than before.

"As I said," Landon said, cutting in, "recruiting."

"I have to agree." Richards prepared to get back into the jeep, or so Shrina thought, but then he opened the back door and pulled out a bound female vampire, holding her half in and half out. "Where were they going to take all of you?"

The vampire grinned and then lunged, only to fall as Richards stepped out of the way and threw her to the ground. He knelt on her back, hand bringing his pistol up to her head, and said, "Talk."

"It's not… as easy as that," the vampire said. "We don't know where. We just… see the calling."

"See the calling?" Richards asked, glancing up with a confused and annoyed look, as if anyone would be able to explain.

"Images," the vampire explained. "Tunnels, a temple… a dragon."

Shrina blinked at those words. She took a step back, confused, and then it was there—the vision of the dragon statue—and she felt a calling, its energy pulling her to it. Instantly she was pulled through the air into a time long ago, riding along on horseback through mountains and stone with a yellow river beside her. Then she was pulled back, up and into the sky.

When she snapped out of it, she was there in Tunisia with her team, staring at this vampire, and they made eye contact. A shared connection.

Shrina pulled up her wrist computer and global map, then spun it until she had the location she recognized from the vision. When she held it out for the vampire to see, the vampire nodded, confirming the location.

"Iran," Shrina said, and turned to go back to her jeep.

"Hold the hell on!" Richards shouted after her. "What am I supposed to make of what just happened here?"

"She told us where they're going," Shrina said. "Bring her. These visions I'm having…" She ignored their concerned look at that. "I imagine the they are going to get stronger the closer we get. It'll be like a game of hot or cold, only she'll freak out the closer we get instead of getting hot."

He glared at her, then walked up and lowered his voice while the others watched with confusion. "Everything okay?"

"Visions," sh said. "Whatever you put in me, it's connected. Now, we can fight it or we can embrace it and go track these bastards down."

After a moment's consideration, Richards

nodded. "Move out," he said to the team. "Looks like we're going to Iran."

Shrina was the first to her jeep, strapping in and sitting back to close her eyes. She hadn't let on, but the fact that she'd had the visions again—and this time, a shared connection with this vampire—terrified her. Her hands were shaking so she clasped them, focused on her breathing, and tried to ignore it all.

Soon they'd have Set and all the answers they needed, and not long after that this whole situation would be put to rest. Until then, she was just going to have to keep her cool and be ready for anything.

19

TRENT: UNKNOWN PLANET B

Trent reclined against the rock walls of the cave, eyes closed while he tried to remember what life on Earth had been like. How long had it been? A day? A year? None of it seemed to matter compared to what he'd discovered there, and yet all of it would be dealt with in time. He'd see to that. Somehow, he just knew.

At one point, he'd made his way back to the crash site to bury the dead. He knew it wasn't practical, but he also knew he had no choice. It was simply something that had to be done. Somehow, after his experience with these two, he no longer worried about the little monsters that had attacked him originally, and as he walked among the little bastards, they ran and hid. He was changed, and they could sense it.

Digging the holes for the graves hadn't worn him out the way it once would have, and he marveled at the way his skin glowed when he was exhausted, a golden steam rising up until he was rejuvenated and could keep going. When it was Enise's turn, he'd taken her body gently in his arms, lowered her into the shallow grave he'd dug, and bowed his head. He wasn't sure if he believed in any higher being, but it felt like the right thing to do. He'd placed one of the spare jackets over her face so the dirt wouldn't get into her eyes. He knew that made no sense, but he was creeped out at the idea of one day being buried only to wake up and find dirt being thrown at his face. He finally scooped the last of the dirt onto her grave, marked it with her Ka-Bar, and then checked the comms one final time just to be sure.

Honestly, he wasn't even sure he wanted them to work but knew it was his duty. Nothing. He stepped back outside the craft and stared out over this world he somehow now belonged to. With a heavy heart, he hoped the sacrifice of his comrades would somehow be worth it, that all of this would pay off and make life better for humanity.

In the meantime, he meant to learn as much about these people as he could. He started walking, wondering if the word "dragon" was more appropriate than "people," or maybe "dragon-shifters"?

Without an alternate, he supposed it fit but imagined there was much more to this story. Perhaps the Earth idea of a dragon came from these people visiting long ago? The search for the answers to such questions was one of many reasons he was eager to return to the cave.

When he'd returned to his new companions, he found them awake and waiting. They asked him questions about his world and listened for hours as he recalled stories of his youth. When they grew tired, they rested, leaving him to his thoughts.

He remembered a time when he'd been a young Marine, uncertain of his future. He'd spent days poring over books, studying, and hours in the blistering heat, exercising to get his body to the next level. Every moment of his life seemed to be leading to the culmination of what came next, or what was falling apart around him. Those were the days when he'd wanted more than anything to be accepted into the space program. That turned out to be even a higher priority than women in his life—a fact that an even younger version of himself would never have accepted.

A sudden shift occurred when the daughter startled, bolting up from where she sat weaving golden strands of light between her fingers. "I hear them."

A moment of silence followed and then a distant roar, barely audible.

"The enemy has returned," the mom said and then turned to Trent, debating. Finally, she said, "Would you like to join us?"

"What? You mean, help with your fight?"

She nodded. "It would mean a great deal and would provide you with a chance to practice."

"Practice what?"

"Your new powers, of course."

He considered this, along with what it would mean to have their help getting off the planet. Everything he'd seen from them so far had been outside his comprehension, and he certainly could use them on his side. Plus, aside from trying to attack him as dragons, they'd been very kind. Maybe he didn't have to leave the planet quite yet but could instead stay and learn.

"Wait," he said and did a double take. "Powers?"

"Join us, and you'll soon see."

With a feeling in his gut that told him nothing would ever be the same again, he slowly nodded.

"Good. Stay close," the mom said, then stood and headed back toward the entrance of the cave.

The daughter lingered, smiling, and said, "I'm Ezail, and my mother is Feras."

"Trent," he replied and then followed her.

Stepping out into the light of day, Trent noted that his eyes needed no help adjusting, which was strange considering they'd just come from a dark cavern. Now that he thought about it, he hadn't needed much help seeing as they walked through the cavern either, though the way in had been dark.

The roar of dragons sounded, followed by a swooshing of wings and a darkening of the sky.

Trent spun, turning to look up as a horde of dragons swept out into the light. While many appeared as Feras had in dragon form, others had thicker scales that were black and glimmered in the sunlight, almost as if they were steel or some other metal. Some had solid bodies while others had spots that appeared to glow green, pulsating with what seemed to be a radioactive flare.

"They're riding out to meet our foe—the group that took you down," Feras stated.

He frowned, confused. "But the red eyes. I thought that was you."

"No, you'll see." She turned to face him, eyes flaring with light. "Are you ready?"

He gulped, confused. "Yes…?"

"Then prepare to grab on."

As he watched, she turned and the gold light flew out of her, engulfing her. First it grew into wings and then expanded until, with a massive roar, she was her dragon self again. Ezail followed suit, and then Feras turned her horned head to Trent and nodded, lowering her neck so he could climb onto her back.

"You've gotta be shitting me," he said and took a step back, wide-eyed. "I don't have a helmet. I don't have a weapon."

Her eyes narrowed and he saw his reflection in them. Even as he watched, the golden light formed a helmet around him, one that allowed full visibility and mobility, and his hands lit up.

Give them a try, a voice said from inside his head.

He didn't understand at first, but then he lifted his hands and pointed them at the hillside nearby. Light pulled from his surroundings, making it darker for a moment, and then a blast shot out like a tier-three plasma cannon, sending debris flying.

"Holy—"

Language, the voice said, and Feras nodded toward her daughter. Was the younger dragon actually smiling?

Trent looked from them to his hands, then back to the spot he'd just blasted.

"I have a feeling I'll regret this someday, but… let's do this!"

He ran forward, leaped onto the dragon's back, and held tight.

As massive wings spread, a flash of panic filled Trent's mind, but by the time he'd registered it, the moment was gone and they were already flying up into the atmosphere. They passed mountains of ice and clouds, and then they went higher still, into the stratosphere and beyond, up past the point where the sky stopped looking orange and everything felt like the clearest night.

Given the clarity of view through his helmet, he nearly forgot it was on. They passed into space and he gulped, panicked that he would suffocate or maybe fall from this dragon and float off.

But as they soared ever upward and found themselves surrounded by other dragons soaring with them, all he could do was whoop out with excitement, all fear replaced by the majesty of the moment. They were immense and majestic, flowing like silk in the wind. Then, all at once, their wings seemed to ignite, the tissue of the lower half of their wings glowing blue and then flaring out, pushing them forward. It was a beautiful sight—so many great beasts igniting like mutated and greatly amplified versions of space fireflies.

There was something else contributing to his newfound sense of security, he realized, and that was the way he seemed connected to Feras. He decided to try to move one of his legs and was surprised to find that it stuck to the dragon's scales like a will-powered magnet. It was moveable but would stick to her unless he wanted it not to.

Save the excitement for when it's over, a voice told him, and he leaned forward, holding tight as his eyes roamed. The horde of dragons continued their upward flight, and Trent rode with his heart thudding and his body feeling more alive than it ever had.

This was what being in the Marines was really all about.

20

SHRINA: IRAN, NEAR THE EASTERN BORDER

"American operations in Iran?" the man said, staring at Richards with bulging eyes. "Are you mad?"

"We're up against a global threat here," Richards pointed out. "One that transcends our two histories."

The man was tall, and his eyes were covered by shades. His Iranian Special Forces gear by itself intimidated Shrina, to say nothing of his six-foot, three-inch muscular frame. A line of Iranian 65th Airborne Special Forces Brigade had come from Tehran to intercept the Americans, and it appeared they had been authorized to use deadly forces.

"Maybe there's no threat," the man said. "Maybe the threat is you."

"You're saying we created these monsters and let them attack our citizens so we could then use it all as an excuse to get a small team of us in through the border and... what?"

"You can use your imagination from there." The man eyed him another moment, then gestured him aside so they could talk privately.

After a moment of them nodding and whispering, Richards waved Shrina over. The others were mostly still in the pods they'd arranged in Turkmenistan, with much hassle. She frowned and complied, all eyes on her in a moment that made her flash back to the memory of being pulled out of the upgrade pod.

"Tell him," Richards said. "He doesn't believe me."

She gulped, knowing it would make her sound crazy. "I saw... a vision, after the enhancements. And then again. All I know is caves, a yellow river..."

"The yellow river?" the man said. "Anything else?"

"No, I mean, well... inside the caves, there was a statue of a dragon with—"

"Glowing eyes," the man said, nodding.

She frowned, waiting for him to explain how he knew that. He was looking back over his shoulder at his team, and after a moment he waved them back. The tension instantly deflated.

"I'm Farhad," he said and thrust out his hand first to Richards, who shook it, and then to Shrina.

"What's happening?" she asked, accepting but

with reservation.

"A bond is forming," Farhad replied with a smile that didn't look exactly natural on his face.

Richards looked as perplexed as Shrina felt as he nodded and said he was happy to hear it.

"You see," Farhad elaborated, "now I know you're telling the truth. I also know that this one," he said as he nodded at Shrina while still addressing Richards, "this one is valuable. How else do you explain that she's had the same visions as the vampires?"

With that, he touched his left lapel and a screen came up in front of him, which he made larger with a gesture of his fingers. There was a line of vampires, all strapped to chairs and all groaning, with red eyes staring straight ahead. One started talking about a dragon and a temple... caverns deep beneath the ground... and following the yellow river.

"Like the yellow brick road," Richards said with a smirk.

"What?" Farhad asked.

"Nothing, just a thing from a classic movie," Richards explained. "How'd you get them to talk?"

"We didn't," Farhad explained. "It just happens, like something's making them do it. Like something's—"

"Calling to them," Shrina finished.

"Exactly." He glanced around at the rest of the

team. "Nobody else has the visions?"

"Not that they've told us about," Richards answered.

"Neither have mine."

"But…" Richards said with a frown, confused. "You haven't had these enhancements somehow, have you?"

Farhad gave him that awkward smile again. "State secret. No comment."

"The pills," Shrina speculated, earning a look of surprised respect from the man.

"Intel?" he asked.

"I was FBI," she explained. "But no, this has to do with my previous experience. I was there when some of the alien tech was stolen, and I was told they'd use it to make pills that gave quick boosts similar to the effects of the enhancements. You're familiar with the side effects?"

The man nodded. "Again, can't tell you anything. Can't confirm I know what you're talking about, but it sounds fascinating."

"Right," she said with a laugh.

"So how do we do this?" Richards asked.

"You follow me," Farhad explained. "We've already managed to figure out the location in their visions within a radius of less than a few miles."

"It's a start," Shrina said.

"Walk with me as we talk strategy," Farhad said, gesturing for Richards to approach their military-grade sand cruisers—essentially a cross between a Humvee and a traditional transport pod, decked out with heavy machine guns and blasters.

Richards nodded to Shrina, who took the cue and headed back over to the rest of their team.

"What's the deal?" Roy asked when she leaned up against the hangar. Getting through the border seemingly unnoticed had been a feat, only to find out that they'd been tracked by special forces and intercepted there. In the end, it had all worked out.

"Looks like we have new friends," she said.

"No way. Tagalongs?"

She explained the thing with the vampires, and he nodded. The others glanced over and listened in.

"My pops would be rolling in his grave," Chung said, shaking her head.

"We want a chance at taking these things down," Shrina argued, "and having some of the world's best at our side certainly can't hurt."

"If they're really on our side," Landon chimed in.

Chung nodded.

Shrina would've loved to argue about it, but Richards had just returned, waving his hand as he said, "Let's roll."

"Destination?"

"We'll follow them, but in case we need it," he said as he pulled up his wrist computer and put in some coordinates, which popped up on the pod's screen. "There you go."

Shrina leaned in to have a look, instantly recognizing the terrain from her vision. This was the place, and it terrified her.

"Looks like you've seen a ghost," Roy said, noticing her expression.

"I honestly have no idea what I've seen," she replied. "But I'm ready to send them to their graves. You can count on that."

"Hell yeah," Landon said, clapping her on the shoulder.

They piled in and soon everyone was rolling out, Iranian and American forces together. As they went, Shrina told her companions the full story about what had happened with her older sister. She told them about how they'd found out about plans for New Origins to attack the governments of Earth and take control, and how Shrina had been the only one they could trust with the info. She continued with how Alicia and Marick had sent her an encrypted message and they'd met up and worked with Trent in Italy to get the information into the hands of the one man they could trust—the Ambassador.

"It sounds so... surreal," Landon said when she'd

finished with the part about finally going to the U.S., only to interrupt an attack on the president. "Straight out of the movies."

"And what we're doing? That's more believable?" she asked.

"None of it is."

"And yet, we're living it." She sighed, staring out the window and hoping her sister was relaxing on some beach somewhere. They passed by cities and rocky hills, watched by herds of goats, and soon they were moving along a bridge that crossed a brown river. Two laughing kids were playing in it.

"I had a sister," Chung said out of nowhere. That was it; nothing else—just the past-tense statement, followed by her leaning her head back and closing her eyes.

"Um, sorry?" Roy said.

Chung opened her eyes and looked at them, scrunching her nose and sighing. "One of the reasons I wanted to serve, actually. One of many, but definitely up there. She'd always talked about going off to join the Army or the CIA—she wasn't sure which but had all these books about each, making sure to do the research before jumping in. That was her way. Spent her whole life researching, only to be taken at seventeen by leukemia… the year before they legalized the cure for it."

"That's..." Shrina didn't know what to say. How could she comfort anyone about that, and did the woman even want comfort from her? "I'm sorry" was all she could think to say.

"My brother wants to go to space," Roy said after a minute. "After what just happened with the attack and everything, I'm not sure how to feel about that. We knew it was dangerous, but..."

"It hasn't changed," Landon argued. "This group attacked. If we stop now or give up on our dreams to go out there, that means they win."

"Sometimes they do."

"That's a shitty attitude," Shrina said. "Sorry, but no, they *never* win. Only if you allow them to, and then it's not really their victory as much as you simply stepping aside."

"Semantics," Roy argued. "And sometimes you have to realize that fighting the fight isn't worth it."

"We're talking about going into space here, right?" Landon persisted. "After finding this gateway on Mars and the ruins, it would be stupid—even negligent—to simply not go exploring."

"Well, maybe I don't want to lose my brother to our quest for knowledge, you know?"

"The apple," Chung said, nodding.

"What?"

"The apple, you know... from the tree of knowledge. Isn't that the biblical story about Adam and Eve?" She shrugged. "I don't know it well enough to know anything, but I think that's what it was about —the evils of going after that which you never needed."

"I think it was more about not doing something if you were told not to," Shrina argued, though she wasn't exactly well-versed in religion either. Any of them.

"Regardless, none of us might be here tomorrow to debate it," Landon pointed out. "Not if we don't have our heads in the game."

"Damn right," Chung said.

"And... that sucks about your sister, Chung." Landon put a hand on hers and squeezed, and she squeezed back. It was a tender moment, Shrina thought, and much too short as Landon suddenly pulled his hand back to grab the wheel and steer, hard, to avoid hitting a goat. "Damn goats!" he shouted.

"Keep your eyes open back there," Richards said through the comms.

"On it," Landon replied, now tightly gripping the wheel.

Shrina's heart was racing, so she leaned back, glancing only once to confirm the goat was okay. It hadn't even noticed.

"We need to keep this light-hearted until we get there," Landon said. "Keep me focused but not distracted. One thing you would take to a new planet if we all had to relocate tomorrow. Go."

"Pecan pie," Roy said without even thinking.

Landon laughed. "Good choice, but not the super sweet kind you get at the generic grocery stores."

"No way. The classy kind."

"We're talking foods?" Chung asked.

"Anything."

"Well, that pie would last maybe a week," she said, running her hand through her hair. She grinned. "Gotta say my little pink vibrating friend."

"Gross," Shrina said, catching on right away.

"I'm not following," Roy admitted, but when Landon laughed and slapped the dash, Roy blushed and said, "Oh… the *vibrating* kind… got it."

"Who knows how much privacy we'd get up there?" Chung said. "And what if all the men died off from some strange disease? Gotta make sure I don't go crazy."

"Shrina?" Landon asked.

"Nu-uh, you first," Shrina replied, still trying to get the image of Chung with a vibrator out of her mind.

"Gotta say my music," he said, holding up his wrist computer. "I've got bands from the past two hundred years on this bad boy. Give us your answer and my reward will be that maybe I'll let you all hear some."

"Like we'd want to hear your busted jams," Roy said with a laugh.

"Just wait. Shrina?"

"Hmm." She really had no idea if she didn't count people. Of course the answer was Prestige, but saying that after Chung told them she'd lost her sister felt wrong, so she said, "I guess my favorite pair of flats."

"Shoes?" he replied with a scoff.

"The most comfortable ones ever. Think about it —you don't know when you'll find new shoes again up there, and those 3D printed ones are horrible. You want to be comfortable in space."

He laughed. "Okay, doable," and then turned on a song. It wasn't bad—upbeat and fun—and soon all of them were singing along with the chorus. Shrina even found herself throwing her head back and letting loose, almost forgetting where she was and enjoying herself.

It wasn't the calm before the storm but rather blissfully riding straight at the storm and not being scared of it—being ready for anything it could throw at them.

21

TRENT: UNKNOWN PLANET B

Flying through space on the back of a dragon was terrifying enough on its own, but Trent was also imagining all manner of alien life forms attacking. On one hand, he felt ready for anything they could throw his way but was equally worried he wouldn't be able to stand up to the challenge. His life flashed before his eyes as he oscillated between the horrible thoughts of floating off alone into space and memories of his dad picking him up and flying him through the living room as a young child, pretending he was a spaceship.

The bliss of ignorance. The joys of youth.

And then all of those thoughts faded, replaced by the knowledge that he was going to die that day because the image in front of him changed as red eyes opened—massive red eyes that took up most of his field of vision. With a sinking feeling in his gut, Trent realized that the dragon eyes he had seen back on the planet were nothing like these. These were much larger, much fiercer.

A nearby dragon opened its mouth. Trent expected fire to shoot out, but instead it was a concentrated burst of bright blue energy. The shot flew at a spot near the red eyes and exploded, and for a few seconds Trent caught a glimpse of their enemy. It wasn't like the dragons so much as it was like a giant snake that worked its way through the sky. Hissing, it lunged for the nearest dragon and caught it in its jaws, crushing it.

Trent sat back, feeling sick.

More attacks came from the dragons, attacks that featured bursts of blue, green, or red energy. The snake moved and flickered back out of sight as it cloaked itself and then opened its mouth to reveal the emerging forms of dozens of ships. These ships were similar to the fighters back on earth, but where the fighters he was used to were shaped like thin arrows, pointing toward their target, these had additional pointers and a more intricate weapons system.

Ezail appeared beside Trent and let out a roar, eyeing him. He had a feeling she was either telling him to stay down or prepare to fight. Since he didn't know which and since he was freaking out at having just seen a massive space snake shooting alien fighters from its mouth, he decided the best course of action was to fight for his damn life. This seemed to be the right choice because more dragons swooped over his head, moving in to meet their enemy. He had seen what his new powers could do planet-side, but he wasn't sure if such a blast would have the same effect without oxygen.

As an enemy fighter zoomed past, unleashing a flurry of blasts at them, one of the black dragons spun and swept it with its tail. Only then could Trent see how massive the black dragons were, even compared to these spaceships. The two dragons he had met were large but nothing like the size of these.

Having knocked the ship off course, the dragon turned and gave chase.

Another alien fighter was coming at them, so Trent hugged tight with his legs while lifting his hands. He focused on the energy as he had done before, only this time the energy was much more concentrated—it shot out like two golden lasers and one hit an enemy ship dead on, causing it to explode completely.

The dragons nearby roared with approval, and then more were attacking. Feras opened her jaw and Trent could feel her power vibrating through his legs. As they swept in again, he lifted himself up, almost standing, and raised both arms to send blast after blast into the enemy ships.

Dragons attacked from all sides, gliding in and out of view. Bursts of energy shot out—some exploding and others coating their enemies in a material that made them start to fall apart even as they flew. Soon the dragons were giving chase as the alien fighters retreated.

Feras turned to her daughter and roared, and the two of them pulled back. They watched the other dragons move on for a moment and then saw the flickering snake in the distance. Then all the dragons were pulling back, too, and Feras was taking him down to her planet. She touched down on the layer of land above where he had first met her and waited for Trent to hop off before transforming back into the humanoid form he had seen earlier. Her daughter followed suit.

"You fought on our side," Feras said with a kind bow of her head.

"He was great," Ezail noted. "We've never seen anything like it."

"You?" he said with a laugh. Everything that had just happened was out of his comprehension, but he knew one thing—if some alien group wanted to hurt these two, he would do anything in his power to stop them. "That was…amazing."

"What you saw was simply a scouting mission," Feras said, "the enemy daring to venture too close to our home."

"Is it… over?" he asked. "I mean, for now?"

She nodded her head, then took her daughter's hand and said, "Come, I'll show you where we live. You did wonderfully, but with a little training you could be unstoppable, I imagine."

He nodded and followed, his mind racing with questions. But as they walked, a terrible dread took hold.

"The humans… my kind. They'll come."

"We trust you'll figure that part out," she replied. "You'll be left with a choice then, a moment that will change your life: Will you become one of us—an emissary from Earth, an ambassador between our two civilizations? Or will you join them if they decide we're a threat?"

"I would never!" He blinked, turned to her, and cocked his head. "One of you? Do you mean… a dragon?"

"Let's not be hasty," she replied with a teasing smile. "But if you prove yourself worthy, who knows?"

That concept was hard to wrap his head around. He contemplated it—his career with the space fleet and all of his connections with humanity… or this, whatever this was. Magic? Super powers like in the old movies? Some new science that he couldn't wrap his mind around? Regardless of the logic behind it, the allure was undeniable.

All he could do was stare ahead in deep thought as they led him off down a path and into one of the tall ice-mountains. Inside, he saw that same golden glow from before, this time radiating from inside the ice walls. What he had thought to be the main habitats of this place must have simply been a forward guard, an outpost. What lay before him now was a glimmering domed city of humanoids just like the girl and her mother—thousands of them. Since arriving on this planet, the question of how to get home had been bothering him, but now that he stood here, staring out in amazement, the question began to fade out of existence. He now saw what he'd been defending when he fought at their side, and he was able to catch a glimpse of what his life could be like here. He would learn everything they'd allow him to learn, training to fight alongside dragons. And one day, perhaps, he would *become* a dragon.

As far as he was concerned, he was home.

22

SHRINA: IRAN, YELLOW RIVER

At long last, the American and Iranian forces pulled to a stop at the edge of a series of rocky, sand-covered hills. Two of the Iranians exited the vehicles first. Camo-covered and weapons at the ready, they took off at a jog, making for the hills.

"Where're they going?" Landon asked into his comms.

"Scouting," Richards said. "You prefer to take their place?"

No response.

"That's what I thought."

They piled out, took a piss break—the ladies going to the other side of the far pod—and then carbed up and hydrated. When they'd finished, they circled up in their respective groups and Richards gave them the simple reminder that this was it—the hunt. They would find the enemy base if there was one, but really, anything was possible, and he had no idea what they might find there.

"If we find a coffin, I'm taking it home as a souvenir," Landon said with a grin.

"Ah, damn," Chung said, pretending to check her pockets. "Anyone have any garlic I can borrow?"

"Hardy-har," Richards said, but he pulled out a clove and winked. "Hey, we don't know what these things are."

"And worst-case scenario, you throw it into your next MRE to add some flavor," Shrina said.

"See, thinking ahead." Richards pocketed the garlic and nodded to Farhad, who was approaching alone.

"Your team ready?" Farhad asked.

"Ready as we'll ever be," Richards replied.

"Right. On my lead." Farhad jogged back toward his men, shouting orders, and then they all fell in behind him, taking off for the hills.

Richards turned back and said, "You heard him. Consider this a joint operation from this moment on. One of theirs is about to get taken down, you do everything in your power to see that doesn't happen."

"I'm not following their orders," Chung said, "just to be clear."

"You have a problem with them?"

Chung glared. "As I said."

"Your orders are to get in there, find the vampires, and kill them. Can you manage that?"

"That, I can do."

"Good," Richards said and then motioned them onward. They took off at a jog in the same direction Farhad and his men had gone, though the Iranians already had a good lead.

They must have charged through those hills for a good hour, but none of them showed signs of fatigue, and all of them were more than ready for the action to start. In fact, Landon let out a whoop of excitement when the first gunshots sounded ahead, and the pace doubled. Shrina was into it, too. They'd made her afraid for her family, and they'd spread terror throughout the world. Now, they were going to pay.

She checked her DD4 assault rifle as she ran, slapped her helmet to ensure it was secure, and called out through her comms, "Make 'em pay!"

Others replied with cheers and calls for blood, and then they were in the mix. Vampires leapt out as if from nowhere, some with blades and claws, and others shot from a distance. Landon charged in with the blade out on his rifle. When he caught his first vampire, he impaled it and slammed it into a rock before gutting the bastard. Shrina was more tactical. Taking a knee, she aimed and squeezed the trigger. The shot hit one of the few vampires with helmets on, blasting through its faceplate and sending blood into the air. Old equipment tended to be weaker, but she had a feeling even hers would give if shot at this distance by a DD4.

A roar came from her left and a vampire materialized wearing an exoskeleton, blue mist vaporizing around him. He wasn't the one named Set, but he'd apparently used the same style of teleportation device, which meant they had more than one. It was time for her to get ahold of that device. As two more vampires teleported in behind the first, she was up, shooting and walking toward them. She paused to throw a smart grenade and then dove. One of them managed to teleport out in time, appearing just behind her as the other two exploded. She was ready, spinning and slamming the butt of her rifle into the vampire's nose. He stumbled back but then spun and hit her with a kick to the legs, followed by a leaping strike that sent a gong sound through her helmet and left her ears ringing.

The vampire grinned, and she realized something was beeping.

"Oh, shit," she said, tearing her helmet off and throwing it at the vampire. He swung, knocking it aside as the explosion went off—enough to shatter the helmet. If it had been on her head, her skull would have been in bad shape.

"A shame," the vampire said, circling her, claws ready.

"You want to play dirty?" she said and let out a four-round burst, then charged. At the last minute she ducked and slid, slamming her rifle right into his groin. As he doubled over in pain, she gave *him* a grin this time and said, "Still human enough for that to hurt, huh? Let's see how you like this."

As she lay at his feet with his head bent over her in pain, she lifted the rifle and fired two bursts, sending eight bullets tearing through his face. The vampire's head blasted apart and he fell, but not before Shrina had a chance to roll aside.

"That's what I'm talking about!" Landon called out from nearby, just as a vampire came at him from behind.

Shrina aimed, fired, and took it down. "Watch your ass!"

"No need when I've got you all over it."

She frowned, not understanding how he could be flirting at a time like this, then motioned to his right where Chung and Roy were battling a couple of vampires. "Shut up and get on them."

He winked and ran over to help. Following close behind, she noted the Iranian forces and other teams, including Richards, clearing a path ahead. There had to be two dozen vampires there, at least, and at least half that number were already dead. From what she could see, one of the Americans was down and three of the Iranians.

"About time," Roy shouted when he saw them, the moment costing him as a shot hit his chest and sent him stumbling back. His foot set down dangerously close to the edge of a drop-off, but Shrina ran to him and grabbed his hand while Chung took out the shooter.

Landon was plowing through the closest group of vampires, but they were giving him hell.

"Thanks," Roy said, recovering and giving her a nod before charging back into the fray.

Shrina stayed close, cautious of being open to shooters now that she didn't have her helmet. Most of the forces ahead were occupied, though, so it was close combat she had to worry about.

When a vampire leaped for her, sharp teeth exposed and wild eyes full of joy, Roy caught him, twisting and slamming him into the ground. Shrina was on it, and as Roy held him down, she pulled her blade and slit the creature's neck.

"Now we're even," Roy said.

"Really? I was the one who killed him."

Roy laughed. "Fine, maybe I'll save your ass again to even the score. We'll see."

They were already moving on to team up against another of the remaining vampires when a loud explosion sounded ahead. All they could see aside from smoke was the guys and gals on their side.

"We've got them on the run," Farhad called out. "Get your team up here!"

"You heard him," Richards said through the comms. "All on me."

The group pushed forward, but Chung had her eyes on one of the vampires and went the other way in pursuit.

"Wrong way, hotshot," Roy called out to her.

"Forget that. This one's mine," Chung called back.

Landon cursed, then pointed up the hill. "You two get moving. I'll cover her."

They were about to argue when Chung cried out, stumbled back, and fell. All three were running for her when they saw cables around her ankles. The vampire ran and jumped over the side of a nearby cliff, and as he went, so did she. Only half-way down he vanished in a blue light and she kept falling.

Shrina felt as if her lungs were collapsing as she watched, trying to think of anything they could do, but even as they ran to the edge of the cliff and looked down, they knew it was pointless. When Chung hit the ground, three vampires converged on her, tearing off her armor and biting into her as shots rained down on them. It was as if the blood they were feeding on counteracted the hits they were taking, and the trio above was in such a frenzy that half of their shots were missing anyway.

"Dammit," Richards shouted into the comms. "What did I say? On me, now!"

But they weren't listening. They wanted their revenge. They wanted their teammate. Shrina was already gauging the distance, analyzing the cliff and looking for a way down, and then she saw it.

"Over here," she said, not even bothering to ask if they were coming. As much as she hadn't been sure she liked Chung, the woman was still a teammate, one of them. This wasn't about to happen without a response.

"What the hell's going on down there?" Richards demanded, but Shrina was already working her way down the cliff. The vampires saw this, and two took off while one grabbed Chung's rifle and started firing up at them.

"I've got you," Landon said, finding a ledge and providing cover fire. "I'll be close behind. Go!"

"You're not as bad as they say," Roy replied, right behind Shrina.

"Shrina…" Richards said, but left it at that.

"I'm not letting them get away," Shrina replied and then turned off her comms.

Soon they reached the base and the vampire wasn't far off, running after his buddies now that he realized he was outnumbered and they'd made it down the cliff. Shrina and Roy started after him with Landon not far behind, they figured. But when they crossed over the next hill, Shrina froze, recognizing the spot from her visions. They'd found it.

The rocky slopes were jagged and covered in salt, with a river of yellow tracing the hills—just as she'd seen it in the vision.

"No need to wait for me," Landon called out from behind, closing on them quickly.

With a quick breath to regain her composure, she pushed on as Landon ran up to the others. They charged through the hills, refusing to give up the chase. The vampire scrambled up the rocks like a damn goat, vanishing over the other side before they reached the top.

"Where the hell…?" Landon said, glancing around.

It was Roy who pointed down to the crevice, just partly visible in the rocks on the other side of a jagged outcropping. They approached, rifles at the ready, and Shrina was the first one to get a good look inside. It clearly went deep, but there was more than just a hole in the ground. Even with the faint light making its way inside, she was able to tell the walls were smooth, carved as if this had been a tunnel or passageway long ago.

With a cautious glance up to Roy and Landon, she knelt down, rifle leading the way, and got a better look.

"Hold on," Landon said, and he tapped her on the shoulder. "Check this out."

She pulled back, stood, and followed his line of sight. He stepped forward so she and Roy followed, and then realized what it was he was seeing. There were larger chunks of rock cast aside, clearly cut, judging by their shapes and edges.

"We're losing him," Shrina hissed. "How's this relevant?"

Landon didn't answer. He simply stared at the ground, then knelt, picking something out from among the rocks. He held up a shiny bit of metal that had letters on it and a half-planet eclipsed by a space station.

"New Origins," Roy said, then whistled softly through his teeth. "What's that doing here?"

"The question," Shrina said as she took it, assessing it, "is why the company was here mining or digging for something."

"You're saying the vampires were here, and they were looking for them all along?"

Her hand went to her mouth. "Oh, no."

"What?" Roy asked, confused.

"You don't think they found vampires and adapted their DNA to, I don't know… genetically engineer the enhancements they've done to us, do you?"

Landon scoffed. "No. That—no."

Roy even chuckled. "As much as I think calling these guys vampires is fun, no way do I believe they're actual vampires of legend."

"I mean, me neither," Shrina said, scrunching her nose. "But… maybe whatever they did find here was part of it. Some other form of ancient material, maybe DNA held for centuries. And since we took what we have after tearing down New Origins, whatever is in these hills might have a connection to how they made us like this."

"Damn," Roy replied, eyes wide and full of curiosity.

"Yeah." Shrina turned back to the hills. "And

someone else tried it, or maybe it's a chemical or some alien star, and it mutated people, creating these vampires."

"That's all speculation," Landon said. "I'm still betting on them being totally separate from our enhancements. I say they came through the gateway."

Shrina nodded. "Either way, I'm guessing the vampire went in here, and I'm guessing there was a reason New Origins was digging in this location."

"So we're going in," Roy said, grinning.

"But not the way they're expecting us." She nodded to the surrounding hills. "If they were digging, I'm betting they found a few tunnels. The one we tracked our vampire to is likely being watched. But if we can find the others..."

It didn't take long, not with the scanning equipment their HUDs provided and the fact that there were red glitches showing up here and there—likely life forms below the ground. The entry they chose was one of three options, not including the first they'd come across. There was one on the back side of the next hill over that had the same well-carved walls and seemed to go in a similar direction.

It took courage, but Shrina entered the darkness. Her mind was racing with thoughts of what could be waiting for her, but stronger than her worry was her desire to see these horrible creatures eradicated from this world. Then maybe her sister and everyone else could continue their lives in safety.

"Tell the others where we are," she said to Landon and then pushed on. Her finger was off the trigger, but she was ready to aim and fire at the first sign of movement.

23

ESPINOZA: SPACE, UNKNOWN PLANET A

The Marines back at the ship met the news with a mixture of gung-ho bravery and the urge to piss themselves. Nobody liked to hear that they had to go try to take parts from a ship that was occupied by some strange mutations being referred to as vampires, especially when a giant sandworm was nearby.

"I saw its mouth," Franco said, shivering next to the fire in spite of the warm air that had taken over.

"When?" Espinoza asked.

"I was falling behind until I saw it." He stared into the flames, mesmerized. "Just for a second, but it was enough to imprint the image on my mind. As the sand cleared… sharp teeth, long like swords. Eyes like the center of the fire here. Pincers if you can call them that. We aren't on some alien planet… this shit is hell itself."

"Corporal," the captain said, scolding him. "People don't need to hear that kind of talk."

"Them or you?" Franco said, suddenly turning on him. "Feeling guilty for putting us in this place? If you're flying—"

WAM! Ellins caught Franco across the jaw with a right cross, dropping him to the ground.

"Enough!" the captain said, and Ellins clenched her jaw, stepping back.

"He was out of line, sir," she said.

"Not as much as you just now…"

Espinoza stepped forward to help Franco up, but the matter was apparently done because the captain turned and stormed off.

"Dammit," Ellins said. "I shouldn't have done that." She turned to the rest of them. "My apologies, but I won't have anyone questioning the chain of command or those in it, not in our situation. Your life might depend on it."

"I deserved it," Franco said, holding his jaw. "And damn, that's some punch you've got there."

"You did deserve it," Ellins replied with a smile. "Doesn't mean it was my place to give it to you. I want to know right now who's in and who's out. If anyone feels safer here, stay. Otherwise, we're going to take what we need, and we're going to find a way to contact Earth."

"Oorah," a couple of the Marines shouted.

"Oorah," Franco said, but he shook his head. "I'm going, Gunny. But that doesn't change what's out there, waiting for us."

"No, it doesn't," Espinoza interjected. "But the fact that it's out there doesn't change the fact that we need their equipment if we hope to get any message at all back to Earth."

"We have no choice," Kim chimed in.

Everyone looked at each other for a moment, then to Gunny. Even Franco seemed to have lost his will to argue. Either that or he'd seen the light.

"Get your belongings and check your gear and weapons," Ellins said. "We don't know how long we'll be out there or what we could run into. I want everyone ready to go in thirty."

"At night?" one of the Marines asked.

"Is there a problem with that?" Ellins demanded.

"It's just... vampires."

Ellins rolled her eyes. "There are no such things as vampires."

"There weren't such things as sandworms before today, either," Kim pointed out.

"And maybe there still aren't," Ellins countered. "Whatever that thing was, the description doesn't sound like what we've seen in movies, exactly. So yes, there's something that only our word "sand-worm" seems to fit. The same with vampires. But I assure you, they don't fly through the night or drain your blood."

"She's right," Kim added. "I mean, they don't die in the daylight or anything like that—a couple attacked us while the sun was still up."

That seemed to help ease the worry of some of the Marines and soon they were getting ready to move out, with only a small contingent staying behind to guard the place. Espinoza checked his ammo and grabbed some more food, then was on his way out when he met Ellins in the doorway.

For a second she moved to get out of the way but then stopped, staring at him. "Something happened, didn't it?"

"Excuse me?"

"Between you two," Ellins elaborated. "You and the corporal."

Espinoza nodded, slowly. "Is that a problem, Gunny?"

She winced at the use of her rank, though what did she expect? She'd been the one to kiss him and then ignore him whenever he brought it up.

Finally, she said, "Of course not. Just want to be sure it won't jeopardize the mission."

"Nothing to worry about in that regard," he said, doubting that was really all there was to the question.

"Right, yeah." She moved out of the way as he did, too, both stepping the same direction and nearly colliding again. For a moment, she looked like she was going to lean in and kiss him, but maybe that was just his imagination because she smiled, stepped aside, and then walked past him.

He wondered what he would have done if she *had* kissed him. Was he now a thing with Kim? They hadn't really spoken about it—not exactly. But now that they'd been so intimate, he sort of wished they had.

Too late now because she was moving back through the ship and two others from the team were walking out. It wasn't like he wanted to pursue anything with Ellins. He had Kim now, or at least he had *something* going with her, but that didn't mean it wasn't all very confusing.

Pushing those distractions aside, he nodded at the Marines and then continued on out the door and into the relative darkness. Several Marines were lounging about, heating up water from their MREs or telling stories too many times repeated.

They weren't two steps out when the first scream sounded—no shots, just a scream followed by a crunching sound. Espinoza unslung his rifle, moved out toward the fire, and joined two others already standing with rifles raised. He hadn't spoken with either of them much, but he knew them as Brown and Christianson, both corporals.

"See anything?" he asked.

Christianson grunted, pointing toward the rear of the ship, off to the right. "Came from over there."

A shape moved and a shadow darted along the ship. Brown opened fire, but it was gone.

"What the hell's going on out there?" Ellins asked through comms.

"Looking into it," Espinoza replied, then motioned Brown and Christianson to move with him. They hesitated but then double-timed it to catch up. Several others were starting to form up nearby, glancing around in confusion.

There was no sign of Kim, but Franco was there.

"Was anyone behind the ship?" Espinoza asked, his voice not too loud.

The group shook their heads, all looking around.

"The captain?" Franco offered.

"Captain?" Espinoza asked into the comms. When no reply came, he said, "Gunny, you seen the captain?"

"Negative," came her reply. "Coming out."

"Roger that."

Espinoza had just turned to Brown when another scream sounded, this time clearly a woman. And if he wasn't mistaken, that woman was Kim.

"Move it!" he shouted, then pointed to Franco. "You all, take a group around the other side. Rifles ready!"

They took off immediately, as did Espinoza and his two corporals. They charged across the dirt, HUDs showing at least three unknowns back there in the form of red outlines moving for them. One was moving fast, leaping up onto the wing of the ship and turning on them. Brown aimed. Espinoza dropped to one knee, preparing to do the same, and then froze.

"Shit, don't shoot!" he called out, turning to stop Brown.

Two shots went off before he could push the rifle aside, and the form he'd seen—Kim—fell. She landed with a thud nearby while two other forms appeared behind her. Espinoza ran for her, shooting like crazy the moment he saw the red of these newcomers' eyes. More shots sounded nearby, but he quickly realized they were from the other side of the ship. How many of these bastards were there?

Kim leaned up from beside him, red bursts

blaring out from her rifle, and then a shout came from Ellins.

"They're in the ship!" she said. "Dammit, where is everyone?"

Espinoza glanced down at Kim, and she nodded. "Go!"

He grabbed Brown and said, "Keep them back, you prick!" and then ran back for Ellins. It wasn't a choice; it was the only move he had. He couldn't leave the gunny alone in there. He came around to the front of the ship and glanced back once to see one of the vampires fall at a shot from Kim. Then they were out of sight.

The door to the ship was clear, but he went in cautiously. "Gunny, you good?"

Her voice was hushed through the comms. "Looking for the son of a bitch."

"I'm with you," he replied. "Just... don't accidentally shoot me."

Outside, the gunshots continued, and there was another scream. It hit him that Kim had been back there with the captain. What could've been the reason for that? It was a dumb, immature thought, he told himself, and he tried to push it aside. Likely, they'd been going over strategy, figuring out the best route of attack—an odd duo to be doing so, but it could've been any number of reasons, and he was letting his mind run wild.

Moving toward engineering, he froze. He'd let his mind wander and it had distracted him. He saw the vampire, only now really believing the term to any degree. It was a man, clearly, with his eyes closed, bending over the form of a limp Marine. The blood dripping down from his mouth and the crazed look in those glowing eyes when he looked up and met Espinoza's gaze—it all said vampire.

Espinoza wanted to scream, but more than that, he wanted to kill the thing. Charging for it, he was surprised by how fast it moved. Even though he'd seen before that they could match his speed, this one had reached him in the blink of an eye. It grabbed him by the neck and lifted, pinning him to the far wall as it drove its claws up into his gut—or would've if not for the armor. Claws scratched and the vampire groaned, letting its claws sink into Espinoza's throat instead. It seemed to be happening in slow motion, but in reality it couldn't have even been a full second since the vampire had snatched him up. Another second like this and it would all be over.

Espinoza thrashed, trying to pry the claws away. Terror threatened to take over as he felt his blood seeping out and saw those red eyes inches from his face. The vampire licked its lips, eyeing the blood, and it was like a new level of rage overcame the beast. Veins appeared on its cheeks and pulsed in its forehead as the vampire seemed to lose all control. It released its grip, going in to drink. Except Espinoza was enhanced, able to recover much faster than others would have been, and he slammed his forehead into the vampire's face.

The beast barely noticed, but it was enough force to leverage the moment. Espinoza got an armored forearm in, slamming it into the vampire's mouth, and growled as he tried to keep the monster off. With the power behind the vampire, it was like pushing against an oncoming car, but then Ellins was there. Slamming her fists into the creature, she grabbed her knife and thrust it up and into the vampire's temple, then kicked its body away.

Espinoza stumbled forward and she caught him, but the fight wasn't over. The vampire leaped to its feet, knife blade still sticking out of its head, and came at them. Together, Espinoza and Ellins unleashed the maximum extent of their upgraded strength and speed, turning the vampire into a punching bag. And when Espinoza managed to bring his knife into the fight, it became a pincushion.

Finally, the vampire stumbled back, fell to one knee, and its eyes started to fade.

"This... isn't us," he said, looking up at them with desperation in his expression, and then his head exploded with a shot from Ellins. She'd found Espinoza's rifle that he'd dropped in the scuffle and hadn't hesitated.

Only then did it register that there were still gunshots and screams coming from outside, along with the war cries of Marines and growling from the vampires. They agreed they needed to get out there and help, as horrible as Espinoza felt and likely looked. Even as he made it back into the night, however, he realized he was mostly healed already.

Brown stumbled past, fell, and stopped moving. He had no gunshots or serious wounds, it seemed, other than shattered armor on his shoulder and arm, and what looked like a nasty bite.

"Over here!" Christianson shouted, and they ran over to where he and Kim—now recovered—were battling off another vampire. Ellins and Espinoza made quick work of it, making sure to slice off the head when they were done in case the vampires' healing powers were anything close to their own.

Footsteps sounded behind them and then grunts. They spun, ready for more action when Franco and two other Marines charged into their line of sight. An orange moonlight shone on their blood-stained armor, but their faceplates were on. Espinoza wished he'd gone back for his helmet before all this had started, but his hand rose to his neck with relief, confirming it was healed.

"We led them right to us," Ellins said, eyes searching the perimeter. "How many down?"

"Four of theirs," Franco said, motioning to the severed head, "counting this one."

"Five," she corrected him. "One in the ship. And ours?"

"Captain Thomas," he said, "along with Alans, Hiriuchi, and Bazel."

"And Brown," Espinoza said, glancing back to see that Brown still hadn't moved. "It looks like."

Ellins frowned, strolling over to the corporal and kneeling to check his pulse. "It's true. But he has no wounds other than the bite."

"I don't like that," Kim stated. "For one, he was bitten saving my life."

"Damn." Espinoza knelt, too, then glanced around into the darkness. "You're saying one bite from these things… and we're dead?"

She nodded. "Maybe. Or maybe this was something else. Who knows? A heart attack? But I'd be willing to bet on the obvious. And since we saw that the claws didn't kill you—"

"Came close."

"But just the fact that they penetrated you," she

finished, "I have to assume it has something to do with their saliva, something related to the bite."

Espinoza nodded, the others watching with a mixture of worry and anger. They wanted revenge but were freaking out as much as Espinoza was starting to.

"We keep our armor on and we're good," one of the Marines said.

Kim cleared her throat, then motioned to Brown. "That happened. The vampire's strength… it's insane when they're in that blood rage."

"You noticed that, too?" Ellins asked.

"Actually," Espinoza chimed in, "the one with us, yeah. It had been feeding on someone inside, and that gave it insane strength and speed. There's something to that."

"It also makes our death count six," Kim pointed out.

Ellins clenched her fists, nostrils flaring. "What do you all say we get off this damn planet?"

"Oorah," a couple of Marines said, not super enthusiastically.

It was time to push back, to make a move on the vampire spaceship and hope to God that the sandworm would let them be.

"Might have to wait a bit," Franco said, pointing to the sky. They all turned to see dark clouds rolling in and lightning flashing—not normal lightning but flashes that, oddly, appeared gold.

"In the ship," Ellins said. "We'll bury the dead when it's passed, then move on to get it done."

They followed her orders, several setting up their weather gear at posts to stand guard but ready to retreat to the ship if it got too crazy. Espinoza hit the head, relieving some of the tension that had built up during the fight, and found Kim waiting for him against one of the walls in the main bay. She motioned him aside and they leaned against the bulkhead, waiting out the storm or for their turn at guard. Others were sleeping nearby, some munching on MRE pound cakes or brushing their teeth. Espinoza chuckled, thinking how, yeah, just because they were all possibly about to die didn't mean they should let personal hygiene go out the window.

Kim pulled one of the folded blankets from her pack and tossed it over them, then laid her head on his shoulder.

"We're really going to get out of here," she said.

"Yes," he said, not sure if he believed it but certainly wanting to.

"If it brought us together, maybe it was all worth it."

He frowned at that. Surely she couldn't possibly mean that getting stranded on an alien planet and seeing their fellow Marines die in combat was all worth it if it meant being with him. That was just wrong.

Her hand found his under the blanket, then gave it a squeeze before she drifted off to sleep.

Ellins walked past on her way to the head and glanced their way. The sight made her pause with a frown, then scrunch her nose and keep walking. Espinoza wasn't sure how to interpret that but knew he didn't want to see a repeat showing on her way back or have her blatantly ignore him. He waited a minute until he was sure Kim was asleep, then moved her hand and head so that she was sleeping soundly against the wall. When he was sure she was good, he stood and walked back toward the main door. It wasn't like the roaring winds would let him get much sleep anyway, so he went to watch the storm through one of the windows.

The attacks were over for now, and they were in a state of relative peace. All was silent but for the roaring winds. Espinoza stared, unable to take his eyes from the sight. There, in the distance, high above the hills among the storming clouds that made day feel like night, was a bright, golden light—not a sun or anything like that, but a golden, glowing figure. It floated there, unfazed by the storm, and then swept away, vanishing behind the clouds.

Ellins was standing nearby, Espinoza realized, and her hand found his, taking it as she turned to look at him. Her eyes reflected the terror he felt.

The situation had just become much more complicated.

24

SHRINA: IRAN, YELLOW RIVER

Even knowing she was faster and stronger than most of the world, to say nothing of her ability to heal, entering the darkness of the tunnel had been terrifying. Shrina led the way, not wanting to use a light and warn the enemy of their approach. It turned out she didn't need to, though, since her eyesight had been enhanced, too. In the past she might only have been able to see vague outlines, if anything at all, but now she had no problem seeing a few feet ahead. It wasn't like daylight, but it helped keep her from hyperventilating.

Tunnel after tunnel led to more tunnels, then stairs or ladders leading down. There was no doubt that this structure had once been much more than simple tunnels. At spots along the way there were fragments of old pottery, an arrowhead merged with stone, and more signs of a curious past. Soon the tunnels opened up into larger rooms, one with arches across the top like an old reception room. Holes and cracks throughout allowed for a dim light so that they were better able to see the room.

"It doesn't look Persian," Roy said in a whisper, staring up at it with awe.

"You're an expert on the matter?" Landon asked.

He shrugged. "No."

Shrina would've laughed if not for the very real threat potentially ready to strike at any moment.

"Where the hell are they?" she asked, moving to the far side of the room, clearing it, and then checking a side room that turned out to be more of a nook than a room. They moved into the nook and kept an eye on the room while Shrina pulled up her wrist computer. She'd set it to track their progress and make a map of the area so far.

"They're probably shaking in their boots," Landon said, holding his rifle tight, ready for action. "Scared out of their minds at the thought of us in their backyard."

Tracing the holoscreen with her finger, she then swiped and nodded. "The tunnel we think he went into should connect at about this point," she said and pinched in, going back to their current location.

"Meaning we keep going. We might have passed any traps or ambushes they set up."

"Or not," Roy pointed out.

"Of course. Be ready. We have no idea what we'll find." Shrina turned back, scanning the areas nearby but finding nothing. "Might all be a wild-goose chase."

"No way," Landon replied. "We've got 'em cornered, right where we want 'em."

She nodded. Sure, why not? Hopefully.

"You know, as a kid I would've loved this place," Roy said.

"What?" Shrina said and let out a soft laugh. "Tell me you're joking."

"Not at all. Dark underground tunnels? What could be better? There were these old Navy bases or something on Whidbey Island up around the Seattle area, and we used to go there every summer to see my grandpa. We'd run around in those tunnels with flashlights, scaring the hell out of each other. You can just keep going down, climbing old metal ladders until it's so dark your flashlight doesn't even pierce the blackness. At least, that's what we thought as kids. Your mind plays tricks on you when you're scared."

"You scared now?" Landon asked.

"Hell no."

"Good," Shrina said, flipping away her holoscreen and hefting up her rifle again. "Then let's go have some fun, shall we?"

"Whidbey Island style?" Roy asked. "I like it."

Again they headed out, this time moving with even more caution because they knew the next rooms and tunnels were closer to the areas that might be more heavily watched. At a turn into a narrow tunnel—the only way to go since the other was caved in—Shrina held up a fist, then knelt to inspect. There hadn't even been any light to reflect off of it, but her enhanced vision had noticed the line. Now, up close, she saw it was a clearly marked tripwire, likely set up to detonate explosives. Something like that going off in there would likely cause a major cave-in, trapping them until they suffocated, if they weren't killed immediately.

She gestured to it, then stepped over with caution.

Her breaths were loud, eyes moving from side to side. Everything felt more real now that they'd seen a modern trap. At the next turn, she pulled back as soon as she'd started to turn the corner. They stood there for a beat, waiting.

"What is it?" Roy asked.

"Something on the wall," she replied. "Might be a mine, the motion-sensor type. I wasn't sure."

"And we're standing here to…?"

"Figure out the next move," she replied. "I'm thinking."

"Throw in our own explosive and set it off," Landon suggested.

"And bring the whole place down on top of us? No thanks." She turned back, analyzing her holo-screen again, and then noticed a pattern. "Look here. We've moved down at regular intervals," she said and moved the map around for them to see.

"Which means there might be a way down just behind us," Roy said, voice heavy with excitement.

"You really are having fun, huh?"

He chuckled. "Near death? Check. Crazy dark tunnels with mysteries? Check. What's not fun?"

"Uh huh." She waved them back, checking their steps, and then paused at a section of the wall that had more cracks than the rest. When she pushed against it, the rocks gave way. She pushed again, revealing an entire doorway. The sounds of rocks falling echoed in the darkness, but no sounds came of the enemy approaching.

Shrina led the way into a small, circular room with a large hole in the middle and stairs leading down along the edges of it. She glanced back, nodded, and began the descent. What she found below caused her to pause mid-step.

The room was round, with a dirt floor and walls that looked even older than the rest of what was above. If all of this had been above the ground at one point, she imagined that maybe this room hadn't been. One wall had been knocked down, however, and abandoned digging equipment was laying against the far wall. In the middle of the room was a structure made of old stone, gray and sandy. It was broken but still clearly retained the shape of an ancient sarcophagus. No body remained, but the earth seemed fresh, and as she drew closer, she saw that it was steaming slightly.

Odd, she thought, until she turned to follow the walls. At that point it made sense because she saw patterns there, patterns she recognized from her vision. Following the wall, she came to a section where the patterns simply stopped, starting up again a few feet later. It wasn't old like the rest of the wall, though it had been made to look like it.

She frowned and tried to break the wall, but couldn't.

"What'd you find?" Roy asked, stepping over.

"This whole room, I think it was a tomb," she said. "And… there's something behind this wall. Something from… my vision."

"The dragon?" he asked.

When she didn't respond, he nodded, then knelt.

"If we apply just the right amount of explosives, we should be able to knock it loose without putting ourselves in jeopardy."

"Check this out," Landon said, not paying attention to them.

Shrina glanced over to see that he'd uncovered some old pottery, probably vessels that had once held treasures meant for whomever had been buried there to carry into the afterlife, depending on the culture he'd come from. But one thing was sure in her mind, and she had to see if they agreed.

"It's like… Mongolian?" she said.

"Not Persian," Roy agreed, applying C4. "As to what from there, no clue. It could be related to the Mongols, sure. Their campaign certainly made it this far."

"Told you," Landon said with a laugh. "Secret history nerd right there."

"Guilty," Roy said. "Fine, I admit it. Whatever. Especially since it seems my nerdiness is suddenly relevant to the mission."

Shrina agreed and moved back to look at the remains of the sarcophagus. It, too, had the horse carvings, faded though they were.

"You know," Roy said, "there're some who say they never found where Genghis Khan was buried."

"It wouldn't have made sense to bury him here, if

that's what you're saying." Shrina glanced up and saw Roy moving back her way, preparing the charge. "I mean, why?"

"Some old ritual?" He motioned to the light steam. "Something they considered magic?"

He could be right.

They called Landon over, knelt for cover, and blew the rocks. It wasn't much but enough so that the three of them could break down the rest. Before they'd even entered, Shrina saw the emerald eyes of the dragon carving staring back at her.

Another vision hit her—one of the dragon coming to life, of it circling her, embracing her, flames engulfing them both… and those flames exploding outward, conquering the world. Everyone dead or kneeling, and she and the dragon standing over them as one.

She snapped out of the vision and nearly choked, her eyes watering and her skin feeling like it was crawling with centipedes.

All of this was too much, too suffocating. Shrina needed air. Her breathing became labored as she tried to figure out what it all meant. Was it some ancient religion that worshiped dragons? Was it somehow related to the Mongols or some other associated group?

"Shrina..." Roy said and turned to her. "I can't believe it. I... I'm sorry for doubting you."

"But what's it mean?" Landon asked.

She stared at the dragon, and she knew the vampires were related. They'd chosen this spot to come together for a reason. They had the same visions as her, but why?

"I'm going to find these sons of bitches and get my answers, dammit." She readied her rifle and stormed back up and then through the tunnels.

She turned her comms on as she walked, meaning to tell Richards where she was and what was happening, but others were shouting, saying they had the vampires on the run, calling for backup. Best to not distract them, she figured, turning the comms off again and focusing instead on accomplishing her part of the mission. One piece at a time, to fix the bigger picture.

At the first corner, she came face to face with a large vampire. He stared at her through one good eye, the other scarred and distorted, and she recognized him from before at the parking garage and the second attack on the launch site.

Feeling furious and wanting answers, she dove into the fight. Bullets tore into his shoulder and she caught him with the butt of her rifle against his jaw, but then he had her. With a mighty heave he held her against the wall, slamming her head against it twice so that she saw spots, or maybe it was simply the blur from his glowing eye. She couldn't be sure.

The others came up behind them, but she held out a hand. "He's mine."

He went for her rifle, and she knew she had him. Focusing on the weapon when the real danger was her—that was his first mistake. She let him have it, then came in with an elbow to his head, knee to his midsection, and a solid punch across his face that knocked him to the floor.

"Why me?" she asked, kicking him solidly across the face so that blood spurted out. "Why were you after me?"

"You still don't know?" he said with a laugh, coughing up more blood. "So... dense."

He caught her next kick, rolling into her so that she was knocked to the ground, and then caught her with two solid punches to her body armor that didn't hurt but made her worry about whether it would hold. Each time, he tried to pull at it, attempting to leave her vulnerable.

"Tell me!" she shouted, grabbing him by the exoskeleton and pulling him into a headbutt.

He fell back, snarling, and repositioned himself into a crouch, ready to pounce. "It's quite simple, really. We have your sister, but she refused to cooperate. With you as leverage..."

"You son of a bitch," Shrina shouted, charging him. He tried to block, but every ounce of her strength was put into those strikes. Two hits and he was down. A third and he was out. A fourth... dead.

She stood there, chest heaving. She was vaguely aware of her companions saying something to her from behind, but she was too focused, too in the zone to hear them. If this vampire had been there, more were nearby. She ran in the direction he'd come from, along a corridor she'd nearly gone through before, when a motion-sensor grenade went off. The explosion threw her sideways so that she hit the opposite wall and fell to the ground. In her anger and haste, she'd forgotten about that.

The world froze, her ears feeling a dull, repeating pain and capturing a distant ringing. All of it came back to life around her as her body started to heal and she realized she was being dragged by two figures. At first, she thought they might be Roy and Landon, but as her head cleared she realized they were wearing New Origin uniforms, not military armor, and they were pulling her by her heels so that her head thudded against the ground as they went.

Bright light—they were outside! She tried to pull back, but one of them turned and kicked her strong enough to hurt through the armor. All she could see was the silhouette of his dark form.

She heard gunshots and her two teammates stormed out, being hit by a barrage of counter-attacks.

A figure was bending over her, and she recognized him—tall, bald, red eyes. His fangs were long and sharp—not so much like a vampire since all of them were sharp. More like… a dragon.

When he thrust down with his mouth spread, she resisted but was still weak from the blast. Teeth sunk into her flesh and she cursed. Her right hand gave up the fight, instead going for her hip and finding the metal handle she'd been searching for. With a whack, she caught him upside the head with her arc baton and sent him stumbling backwards. She turned to see Roy in the midst of hand-to-hand combat with one of the vampires. His weapon had been knocked aside and Landon was trying to get to him. He shot two vampires and spun to shoot another, then turned back to one of the first two as they healed and came for him again.

They were outnumbered, and she'd been bitten. That realization hit hard as she turned and went for him again, the vampire who called himself Set. There was no question in her mind—she was going to die, and most likely it wouldn't be long now. And since that was the case, she might as well take as many of them with her as she could.

Bursts of electricity shot out as she caught Set a second time with the arc baton, and he staggered back, cursing.

"Where's Alicia?" Shrina asked, preparing for another strike. "Where's my sister?!"

She lunged, but he was fast. Eyes glowing even brighter with the fresh blood in his system, red veins bulging, and muscles becoming even tauter, he threw himself sideways and came at her. She dodged the strike, growling. When she struck again, he rolled out of the way and came up with a kick to her knee that ended in a loud pop and sent her to the ground in pain.

Her rifle was there and she lunged for it, but Set also lunged, landing beside the rifle and grabbing her wrist with one hand while slamming his forearm into the back of her elbow with the other so that he snapped that, too. Pain shot up her arm, and then the shock of getting hit on her knee was gone and the pain from that was strong, too.

Normally she'd push through it, knowing she was going to heal anyway and that it was all temporary. But not this. She was crippled, about to die, and… helpless. Her eyes rose to meet Set's and she growled, trying to pull on any reserves she had left.

She knew that if she failed here, Alicia would be in trouble. They had her, and now it was up to Shrina to set her free. If she could just make it long enough for her body to heal, she might have a chance.

Pushing through the pain, embracing it as a reminder of how desperately she needed this, she took advantage of the fact that he was still holding onto her broken arm. She pretended to try to pull away, and when he resisted, she relished the smug grin on his face as she pulled back into him, using her good leg to kick out his lower half and roll him onto the ground as she pounded her head into his face. Two times she made contact. Her head felt like it was going to burst, but already the pain from her arm and knee were less and she was given an extra burst of energy as she threw her elbow into his face for the third strike.

The fourth, however, never landed. As she came back in with her elbow, a vampire plowed into her side, knocking her over. Set was up before she could even realize what was going on, and then Roy was there, rifle in hand, sending four-round bursts through Set and the other vampire. Set spun, activating part of his exoskeleton so that it glowed, and then a blue energy shield formed between him and Roy.

Not another glance was given to the other

vampire as Set came back for Shrina. Roy shouted and charged. Set caught him by the throat and tossed him overhead as if he weighed nothing. Shrina turned with horror to see her friend—a man she had only recently considered going on a date with—slam head-first into the nearby rocks.

She came at Set again, or tried. Two steps into her attack, she stumbled, felt her head rolling, and collapsed to the ground. Her stomach clenched as pain took hold of her entire body from the inside, working its way out. Like a flame moving through every cell of her body, the pain burst forth and consumed her in its entirety.

Her screams echoed off the rocks. Only a distant awareness of Landon was present in her mind as her eyes lost sight for a second, then returned to see red splotches and him charging. Darkness took over and then she was back, watching him there in front of her, only she realized that his eyes were staring back at her with no life to them. Then she realized that his head was on the ground, his body still falling behind it, all in slow motion. Darkness again.

The pain stopped, but she couldn't move. Her eyes wouldn't open, and only the taste of blood on her tongue—likely from biting it with the pain—served to tell her she was alive at all.

"Leave the bodies," Set's gravelly voice said.

"And her?" one of the others asked.

"She's no use to us now."

As the sounds of heavy breathing and footsteps faded, so did Shrina's awareness and her last moment of life.

Nothingness…

Death.

Empty…

Nothingness.

She was dead. Everything told her so, except… why was her mind working? There was a movement in her chest and then breath flooded in and she was awake, eyes flashing open. With a gasp for air, she reached out, fingernails scraping a hard rock surface as she pulled herself up.

Her head was pounding and her mind reeling. Could this be an effect of the bite? Some sort of outbreak the vampires brought with them? A glance around showed that she had fallen from the ledge above when Set got her. They'd likely left her corpse, assuming she was gone like all of their other victims —one bite to someone modified and they were gone.

But not her.

Landon's head was there on the ground, his body a few feet off. Roy was crumpled up against the rocks. If she was alive, why not him? She stumbled over, dropped to his side and pulled him over, trying not to see the lifeless eyes or the protrusion from his neck. Apparently, this wasn't a wound one could heal from.

Slowly laying him on the ground, she looked at him one moment longer, thinking what might have been, and then stood.

Something moved in the shadows and she turned, hissing. The reaction didn't make sense but felt natural. She blinked, trying to process, and wondered why the shadows were fading before realizing that they weren't, but her eyes were seeing through the darkness.

Nothing was there. Or… nothing she could see.

With a step forward, she crouched, preparing to pounce, and held her hands out for the attack. Long claws grew from the tips of her fingers, and she stared in confusion. Was she one of them—a vampire? Even though she knew they weren't really vampires, everything she'd learned in the caves told her there was something to them—something mythical.

As she stared at her hands, the transformation continued. Her skin grew scaly and small horns grew out of the ridge of her forearm. She took a step back as if she could escape herself and then roared into the sky.

None of this made sense. She couldn't be one of

them, and deep down she knew that she really wasn't. She was something more, though she didn't quite understand what yet. All she knew was that she wouldn't let this stand, that she'd go after them and teach them a lesson. She'd have her justice, her revenge, her taste of victory as she tore them apart.

It couldn't happen fast enough. A yearning rose up inside of her, a craving for blood and violence. She longed to be tearing her enemy to pieces, and that's when she felt the pain tearing through her back. It originated at her spine, surged up into her shoulder blade, and then burst out. No, it wasn't pain that had burst out, she realized, but… wings.

At that revelation and the swooshing of her own wings, she looked down and saw the ground disappear beneath her as she rose higher. Her long, black wings spread out on each side, with hooked horns at the peak of each. Deep within she knew this should be freaking her out, yet she also knew it was right.

As images flashed through her mind, something called for her. She realized it was the carving of the dragon with its glowing eyes, and she thought only of destroying those who had hurt her, those who had killed her friends. It was time to hunt those bastards down. It was time for justice.

She flapped her wings and took off into the sky, ready to make her enemy pay.

AUTHOR NOTES

You have now finished the first book in my Ascension Gate series. What did you think? Did you know that it's related to my Biotech Wars books? You don't have to read those and I don't consider them prequels, exactly, but they've been referred to as my *The Hobbit* if this series is my *The Lord of the Rings.* What that means is—this book, and the Ascension Gate series—have been long in the making. My wife and I outlined this series a while back, spending our date nights or lunches going over story ideas. What you've seen here is just the introduction. We've barely cracked the surface, and all that juicy fun stuff will be following in coming books.

So what's it all about? I see this as my version of a SciFi superhero story, told in a sort of space fantasy way. What is the difference between a superhero story and magic? Someone answered that superheroes have their powers from genes or mutations or something like that, while magic is learned. That doesn't seem to be true in every situation. Honestly, I'm not sure what the difference is exactly, but I'm going with the idea that what we saw with Trent is more similar to the situation with the Fantastic Four or other superheroes who got their powers from exposure to some element or explosion or things like that. We saw something happen with Shrina at the end too, and will get into what that really is and means in book two.

What about... wait for it... the vampires? As you've probably guessed, they aren't *really* vampires. They are called vampires because most humans don't know how else to accept them. People who have read my other books—and maybe some who haven't—likely know what they are and where they come from. If not, keep your eyes out for book two, as it'll be discussed there.

All of this ties together in a way that excites me as a storyteller and I hope excites you equally (or even more). I already have the next three books outlined, but I'm not going to rush them. I'm going to have fun, writing them as the stories excite me. So stay tuned, and please check out my other books in the meantime. Also, I would greatly appreciate it if you can leave reviews. Thank you!

Justin

JOIN THE NEWSLETTER

And join the FB group!
https://www.facebook.com/groups/JustinSloan/

PREQUEL SERIES - SAMPLE

None of the red dots on Stealth's HUD would be alive in a few minutes, so he had no reason to worry.

No, it wasn't worry that crept up on him, sending the taste of bile into the back of his throat and a building tension in his chest.

What then, he wondered as he lifted his rifle and prepared to breach Subsection Alpha of Space Station Horus's living quarters. This was a known hangout for the lowlifes of this place, and rumored hiding spot of the hacker group that called themselves "The Looking Glass." His target.

This wasn't Stealth's first mission, so the reaction his body was having to it didn't make sense. A glance at Red showed that the man was ready, breaching charge in place and hand up. He stared back through his faceplate—full, to protect against explosions. It reminded Stealth of a bug, with its built-in air filter in case of gas attacks and the small antennae-like horns on the top and rear, similar to the helmets they'd worn in their Marine Corps days.

Stealth did his best to push the unsettling feeling down, focusing instead on a memory of his training in the Marines before coming here. A drill instructor back on Earth, standing before him in his body armor of green and black, shouting at him to do just one more pushup, then another, then another. "Just one more," and it went on and on. Repetition, something familiar… order to the chaos. That memory always calmed his nerves, though he was certain it had been the source of an opposite reaction at the time.

Since it was one of his few remaining memories, he clung to it like a dog with its favorite chew toy—which happened to be another snippet of a remaining memory, though one he relied on far less often.

Here on Space Station Horus, he was part of something bigger, part of something new. He and Red were elite soldiers in Project Destiny, a special team within the privatized military that controlled the space stations. Being part of this team meant they had special equipment, special biological enhancements, and special privileges.

However, it also meant that his team was the target of The Looking Glass, which made the terrorist hacker organization their main enemy. If Alice or any of the other top marks were here, he was sure as hell going to take them down.

"You with me?" Red's voice came across their private comms, a direct channel just for him. As if he needed that now too. Babying.

"Breach."

"Are you—"

"Just breach already." Stealth readjusted his shoulder rifle, securing it in place against the section of his exoskeleton that allowed for maximum mobility while adjusting for kickback.

Red shrugged, triggered the breaching charge, and rolled back against the wall, out of the way. Three, two, one… KABOOM!

The door blew off its hinges, showering debris inward. A cloud of dust rose up around the two soldiers as they entered. Oddly, the HUD screen showed more red dots than could be possible—hundreds of the enemy in here, all armed to the teeth. So much that it was obscuring his vision, one of the problems with these damn devices. Red was already shooting, but Stealth took the time to turn off his display.

Instead of a room full of enemy targets, all he saw was his partner, the cloud of dust, and three people huddled in the corner. Movement flashed, and he registered a fourth person who came swinging in from his right.

At least he hadn't been wrong about something feeling off with the mission, he thought as the large technician plowed into him. Thanks to the exo-suit and its enhanced abilities, he resisted the attack, but the hit did cause him to drop his rifle.

One man was down, and Red was moving on another, shots ringing out. Then a hand was reaching for Stealth's rifle. Still wrapped in combat with the first attacker, Stealth let his training and enhanced speed and strength take over. When the man pulled back for a punch, Stealth moved to the outside of it, caught the incoming arm, and twisted it around before kicking out the man's knee with a loud pop.

The hand was on his rifle now, so he slammed his attacker into the nearby wall, headfirst, and spun to get his weapon back.

But the hand belonged to a young, teenage girl. She had the rifle, but was unsuccessfully trying to lift it. Without the genetic enhancements of PD, that would be tough. Tears in her eyes, she was staring at the now unconscious man on the floor.

"The hell did you do to my dad?" she yelled, then pulled the trigger even without the gun fully raised.

A four-round burst shot out, three rounds planting in the floor and one going on to ricochet around the room and off Red's body armor. Red turned to fire on her in retaliation, but Stealth leaped, knocking him sideways. As soon as he'd recovered, he turned back to the girl, reached her in two strides, and snatched away the Destiny's Destroyer Assault Rifle—DD4, as they called it.

"Cease fire!" he shouted to Red, then pulled up the comms in his helmet. "Stand down. All teams, stand down. We've been had."

"Negative on that," Captain Legorn's scratchy voice replied. "All teams, prepare for new assignments."

"What the hell's going on?"

"Sergeant, you were not given authorization to shut down your helmet during combat," the captain replied, reminding Stealth why he disliked the man so. "Luckily for us, Red follows orders. Even more luckily for us, everything's going to plan. Now stand by for orders."

Stealth looked back at the girl, kneeling beside her father now. He was awake, at least, which was more than could be said for the worker Red had put a bullet in. Dammit, what kind of horror storm was this?

"New coordinates incoming," the captain said. "Proceed."

"Roger that," Red said, having recovered and now glaring at Stealth with his mask raised. Cutting off comms, he added, "Stick to the program, hot shot," then slammed his mask back on and headed for the far door.

They moved through the door and into the next corridor, an empty hallway with eerie yellow lights flashing overhead. Metal beams ran across the side of the walls, with empty patches revealing the hallways on each side. Likely under construction, and just as likely to never be fully completed, as was the case with much of this station. Money was better used for military expansion and defenses, even if extraterrestrial life hadn't actually been discovered yet.

And since Earth had begun diverting large amounts of its resources into terraforming, the space stations weren't receiving subsidies anymore. It was easy to understand why the people were fighting back, angered by their low wages and cutbacks on rations to the lower crust.

"What are we doing here, Red?" Stealth hissed over their private channel. "They said to get in, hit the target, and get out."

"Remembering that I'm not the target, right?" Red replied, ignoring the question. "Just want to make sure."

"Dammit, you saw that girl back there. You were just going to shoot her, too?"

"I get the job done," Red growled. "Some teenager chick has my partner's rifle, I take her out. Man up, bro."

The words irked Stealth to a whole new level, but as he was about to respond, a new direction showed up on his screen. They turned, the captain starting to shout at them through their comms that they were going the wrong way, and then—KABOOM!

As the floor disappeared beneath them, Stealth found himself reaching, arms flailing as he dropped his rifle and tried to catch hold of something, anything. He was falling, darkness consuming him. Then another explosion went off, and he was vaguely aware of Red's helmet flying past, above.

Helmet... maybe? In the flash he realized that there might have been more than helmet there. No torso, but more than helmet.

The floor below slammed into him with a shock that shot through even the exoskeleton-reinforced body armor. He froze there, back arched and chest feeling like it would explode. Shooting pain held him in place, coursing through his limbs and wanting to fly out with a yell of agony, but he gritted his teeth and refused to give them that satisfaction.

Whoever had done this to him and his partner had just made a horrible mistake. He would heal. He would find them. He would take them down without mercy.

But first, he had to get out of there before more attacks came. With a growl, he staggered to his feet, noting that the exoskeleton was bent and his shoulder dislocated.

He positioned himself against the wall and threw his shoulder into it, screaming now, unable to help it. A glance around showed no sign of attackers, so he took another moment to disconnect the exoskeleton on his upper right side, where the dent and injury were.

A buzzing was coming from his helmet, so he hit it with the palm of his gloved hand. His ears rang, and then a moment later he heard someone shouting for him and Red.

"Stealth here," he replied. "Red… is down."

A brief silence followed, during which Stealth started to back away down one of the dark chambers. Whatever came next, he certainly wasn't going to be found sitting around, waiting.

"Stealth, is that you?" Captain Legorn's voice came in over the comms.

"Yes, sir."

"Get the job done, and we'll get you out of there," Captain Legorn commanded. "Stick with the plan, soldier."

Soldier. Huh. As much as that was true now, his being a part of Project Destiny, he knew in his heart where he belonged. This feeling of unease and suspicion had never been with him back on Earth, back when he was with the Marines. He didn't remember a whole lot from those days, but he remembered that much.

"I'm a Marine, dammit," Stealth replied, turning to abandon his mission and return to the command room. He meant to find out just what the hell was going on here. While he was at it, he would see that Captain Legorn got a piece of his mind.

(Read More...)

WHAT NEXT?

Thank you for reading STAR FORGED. Please consider leaving a review on Amazon and Goodreads, then grabbing book two soon!

Did you know that the Ascension Gate series has a sort of prequel trilogy? You don't have to read it, but if you want to see some of the events that happened before this book, check out the BIOTECH WARS, starting with PROJECT DESTINY.

The audiobook is narrated by Adam Verner!

Terraforming on Mars leads to the discovery of old

ruins, followed by an alien tech that will change everything. This is only the beginning.

Space Station Horus faces a conflict between supersoldiers and hackers.

Alice was told that her husband was dead, a month after he went up to space. Now she's formed a team of technical assassins dedicated to taking down New Origins, the corporation in charge of the station, if she doesn't get answers. Someone has to hold them accountable--even if it means going up against an army of genetically engineered super soldiers.

Stealth is an elite among elites. This Marine wanted to be on the front line of expansion into space, and now he is. Only the hacker organization known as The Looking Glass stands against them, trying to pull apart all of his team's progress, all they believe in.

Neither will stop until they have justice.

Made in the USA
Las Vegas, NV
16 February 2022